BRIGHTSTAR FILMS INC.

PRESENTS

TRIPLE 'O' SEVEN

A MAJOR MOTION PICTURE SCHEDULED FOR WORLD WIDE RELEASE 1990.
BASED ON THE BEST SELLING BOOK
"TRIPLE 'O' SEVEN"
BY IAN JAMIESON
PUBLISHED BY
THE MYSTERIOUS PRESS.

Screenplay Ian R. Jamieson
Producer Anthony Kramreither
Associate Producer Orval Fruitman

TRIPLE 'O' SEVEN

A Novel By Ian R. Jamieson

Screenplay Ian R. Jamieson

TRIPLE-O-SEVEN

IAN R. JAMIESON

THE MYSTERIOUS PRESS

New York • London
Tokyo • Sweden • Milan

MYSTERIOUS PRESS EDITION

Cover design by Harold Nolan
Cover illustration by William Sloane/Three

Mysterious Press books are published in association with
Warner Books, Inc.
666 Fifth Avenue
New York, N.Y. 10103

A Warner Communications Company

Printed in the United States of America

First Printing: March, 1990

10 9 8 7 6 5 4 3 2 1

Dedication

This book is dedicated to my father, from whom I inherited my bizarre sense of humor; to Baron, for his help; and to Brittany and Brandy, who in their unique way provided an inspiration. I would also like to dedicate this book to all those who helped and believed in Triple "O" Seven. In particular, Karl Siegler, Otto Penzler, Coranne and Ray Anderson, Colin Skinner, Kim Middlestadt, Bill Malloy, Gary Fisher, Ron Goulart, Geraldine Spinella, George Donaldson, the Prime Minister of England, the Queen and Prince Philip for inviting me up to the palace, British Intelligence, and the President of the United States—who also gave me not only inspiration, but also the ability to laugh at everything.

Chapter 1

BARSETSHIRE, ENGLAND

The first assassination attempt occurred before he knew he was a secret agent again.

That was during the annual fund-raising fete on the vast sprawling grounds of Kingsley Academy in the spring of this year. The day was chill and overcast and a sharp wind came blowing through the cedars, birches, and limes that surrounded the rolling lawns and sturdy, ivy-covered last century buildings of the school. The bright striped tents fluttered in the wind, at least three of the boys had their distinctive blue and gold caps snatched off and carried away across the gray afternoon, and the bishop's plump wife was growing increasingly uneasy about the leaves and bits of twig that kept blowing into the large punch bowl of pink lemonade she presided over.

"There it is again," old Leslie Pimpernel was saying. "I'm certain."

"I don't hear a thing," responded Triple 'O' Seven, a tall, lithe man with dark hair and matching mustache. "Didn't hear anything at the pie and cake bazaar either."

He and the gaunt tweed-clad headmaster of Kingsley were now standing near an outdoor jumble table.

"Would've sworn something dangerous was ticking away inside that marble fudge cake." The headmaster licked away the last dab of brown frosting from his thumb. "But now I'm dead certain I hear a telltale ticking here in the vicinity of this concession, Seven. Tick tick tick—that sort of sound." Hunching his narrow shoulders slightly, he scanned the array of white elephants spread out on the rickety table. "Just exactly the sound a time bomb traditionally makes."

"Usually these days, sir, you aren't aware of any sound at all." Seven glanced around at the crowd on the lawn. "Until the explosion."

"Just might be concealed in this bust of Winston Churchill," Pimpernel said, pointing. "Be ironic if one of . . . Ah, no, make that two of Her Majesty's crack secret agents were carried off by an infernal device concealed inside a—"

"We're former agents," reminded Seven, glancing around once again.

Gingerly the headmaster lifted up the bust and held it to his ear. "Very realistic cigar, isn't it? Ah, but the ticking is not emanating from within."

"I thought you'd long since recovered from that spell of jitters that caused them to suggest you retire from Special Intelligence and return here to—"

"Jitters, old man, and an instinct for self-preservation

are not the same thing.'' Headmaster Pimpernel very carefully lifted up a vase that had *Souvenir of Brighton, 1946* painted across it. ''Once out in Singapore, they used a vase such as this to sneak a—''

''What was a *Souvenir of Brighton, 1946* vase doing in Singapore?''

''Wasn't identical to this one, old man, just deucedly similar.'' He listened to the vase for a moment, then peered inside it and shook his head.

''Don't let the price tag bother you, Mr. Pimpernel,'' said the lean woman behind the table with a smile. ''We're always willing to bargain.''

''How's that? Ah, no . . . no, I'm not actually interested in purchasing this. It merely had set me to thinking back to a grand time I once had in the vicinity of Brighton.''

Taking the headmaster's arm, Seven urged him a few feet away from the table. ''Neither one of us is important to anyone anymore,'' he told him, grinning. ''Certainly not important enough to be murdered in the very middle of a school fete.''

Pimpernel sighed. ''Perhaps not,'' he admitted reluctantly. ''And yet, Seven, I've had the damndest feeling ever since I awoke that something is amiss. Ah, but that well may be simply because I loathe these fund-raising events so thoroughly.''

''I find that if you approach them with—''

''I continue to miss, I fear, the excitement of the secret agent life,'' said Headmaster Pimpernel, sighing once more. ''In your father's day, Seven, when he and I faced many a formidable—''

''That's all in the past, sir. As is my own career with

Special Intelligence,'' he said. ''I've now settled in to teaching here at Kingsley. I'm very near to being content with my lot in life.''

''Yet it's a damned shame that a man with your abilities, and your lineage, should've been put out to pasture for such a trivial infraction as losing a battleship. I mean to say—''

''Didn't actually lose it, sir,'' corrected Seven. ''Everyone knows exactly where the thing is—at the bottom of the Caspian sea. But retrieving it simply proved to be a bit too expens—''

''And that cargo plane you lost in the Himalayas''—the headmaster gave a shrug—''really wasn't worth more than a few million pounds . . . Or was that simply misplaced like your battleship?''

Seven shook his head. ''No, the cargo plane was actually lost. Vanished.''

''Well, that's an easy thing to do in the Himalayas, with all those beastly mountains and the snow.''

Seven said, ''I see someone I ought to speak with. If you'll excuse me, sir.''

''Ah yes, go along.'' He made a dismissing gesture with one lean hand. ''I believe I'll trot back to the jumble table and have another go at locating that bomb.''

Emily Watts-Batsfree took three steps out of the peppermint striped tent. ''How decidedly odd,'' she remarked, pressing slender fingers to her lips.

''Hmm?'' inquired Seven, who'd spotted her entering the fortune telling tent a few moments ago and headed this way as soon as he was able to elude Headmaster Pimpernel.

''It's only that Madame Esperanza, which is what Mrs.

Berrilsworth likes to call herself on these occasions, just now predicted that I'd be meeting a dark handsome man,'' said Emily, smiling at him. She was a slim, young blonde of twenty-five. ''And here I am running right into you.''

''Fate obviously. Mightn't I buy you tea at the—''

''Of course, Madame Esperanza's prediction was that the dark handsome man would be much swarthier than you, not taller that five foot four and wearing a sombrero. Still, though, that's not a bad prophecy for someone who's using an inverted fishbowl for a crystal ball.'' Smiling again, she took his proffered arm.

''Uncanny, especially since I only just now donated my sombrero to the jumble—''

''Don't tease me, Trip.'' They began walking across the grass together. ''I happen to be sincerely keen on things supernatural.''

''A family trait.''

''No; Father, being the Vicar of St. Bardolph's is much more conventionally inclined.''

''Tea?'' he asked again.

The wind was growing stronger, more persistent. It worried at the skirt of Emily's pale blue spring dress. ''You like baroque music, don't you?''

''Dote on it. Even whistle it in the shower every morning, which you'd know firsthand if you'd accept my invitations to—''

''I simply don't want to get involved in any new intense relationships just yet,'' she said as she tugged him in a southerly direction. ''The last time that happened I ended up stranded in Yugoslavia. My fault, really, for falling passionately in love with an acrobat who—''

"The refreshment tent is yonder," he mentioned, pointing in a direction opposite to the one they were heading in.

"True, but the Baroque Quintet is playing in that attractive yellow and green tent over there."

"You're intending to inflict it on me right now?"

"In approximately five minutes, yes."

He nodded. "All right, but after that you have to—"

"No, after the concert I really must take over the running of the pony ride so that Googie Warriner can—"

"Very well, I withdraw the invitation, and am assuming a hangdog expression."

She studied his face for a few silent seconds. "I'm well aware of your reputation as an international romantic figure, Trip, and I realize that my refusal to—"

"You're confusing me with my father. My romantic career, while serving my country, was rather limited and drab."

"Three hundred and eight women isn't exactly my notion of limit—"

"Where'd you get that number?" he asked, frowning.

She looked away, the wind fluttering her long blond hair. "Some scandal sheet I imagine, one that Cook was reading."

"Well, everyone knows that they tend to exaggerate."

"Even if they'd doubled the number, it's still an impressive amount of conquests for—"

"Not by secret agent standards."

Emily produced two crimson tickets from a supply in a pocket of her dress, handed them to the bundled-up old gentleman standing beside the tent opening. She led

Seven inside the music tent. ''We'll have our choice of seats.''

There were six rows of folding chairs arranged on the grass, facing a low makeshift bandstand. Except for a plump woman in a green coat who was dozing in the third row, the tent was empty.

''Baroque hasn't been doing well on the charts lately,'' mentioned Seven, escorting Emily to a front row seat and settling in next to her.

''We're doing much better than this on the ring toss, and that's the least popular booth.'' A frown touched her forehead as she looked around the tent.

Off in the woods a deep rumble of thunder boomed, then two more. The canvas walls of the tent shuddered. More thunder, rolling nearer. The first heavy raindrops hit the striped canvas.

Seven popped to his feet. ''Well, I imagine they'll cancel now on account of—''

''No, here they come.'' She pulled him back down beside her. ''Don't let's leave, Trip. The poor ladies'll be disappointed if they don't have anyone awake in their audience.''

''Rather imposing ladies, aren't they?''

The quintet was made up of burly, thickset women in white party frocks. They came stomping onto the wooden stage, using a flap at the rear of the rain-beaten tent. Each carried a black instrument case.

The burliest, thickest of them stepped to the rim of the platform. ''We'll begin with a Vivaldi medley, ladies and gents,'' she announced in a croaking voice. ''Just as soon as we get our instruments ready.''

The lute case contained an Uzi semiautomatic carbine, the mandolin case held a Bushmaster automatic rifle, and the other cases produced similar weapons. In less than a minute all five were swinging up to aim directly at Triple 'O' Seven.

Chapter 2

Swiftly Seven shoved Emily toward the ground, thrust his hand inside his blazer, and grabbed for the Baretta pistol in the shoulder holster he still wore from force of habit.

As he started to lurch free of his folding chair, it made a snapping noise and tried to shut on him.

This caused him to go tipping over sideways down onto the grass.

Several slugs chuffed through the air where he'd been seated earlier.

Emily, meantime, had whipped her skirt up, yanking a Glock 17 automatic pistol free of a thigh holster.

She went rolling over the grass and then, rising deftly into a crouch, fired three rapid shots at the lady baroque musician who was brandishing the Bushmaster automatic rifle.

Emily's second shot took the woman in the chest, causing her to go dancing backward across the wooden planking of the stage. The Bushmaster discharged into the sagging roof of the music tent.

Rain came rushing down through the fresh rents in the canvas.

The Uzi was eating up the sward all around the sprawled Seven. Getting his pistol out, he fired twice as he went scooting toward the second row of chairs.

He winged the lady with the Uzi. She dropped her weapon, yelping and hopping.

"Not bad," observed Emily, bringing down the cellist and then the violinist.

"Crikes," exclaimed the second lutist. She spun on her high heels, ran across the stage, and dived out into the rain through the rear flap.

"Stay here where it's safe," Seven called to Emily as he went off after the runaway lutist.

"My," remarked the woman in the green coat, wide awake now, "this is a much livelier sort of concert than I'd anticipated."

The rain was falling more heavily, the wind was fierce.

A blue and gold cap came sailing by, nearly slapping into Seven as he ran in pursuit of the fleeing assassin.

The crowd was thinning rapidly, most of them heading for shelter indoors.

"I say, Mr. Seven, sir," called a gawky youth, "I don't suppose this is an apt time to introduce you to my mum, is it?"

"Not really, no, Sidgwick," he agreed and kept running, feet splashing up mud.

A great gust of wind came rushing at him and the galloping lutist. It tore the gray wig right off the assassin's head, carried it right smack into Seven's face.

Momentarily blinded, he stumbled over a tent peg. He sprawled against the side of the fortune telling tent.

As the canvas structure collapsed around him, Seven fell against the card table in the center of the floor. The heavy upside down fishbowl atop the table flipped up into the air, spun twice, and landed with a resounding thunk atop his skull.

He managed to rise to one knee before passing out.

There was a fire crackling nearby.

Triple 'O' Seven awakened.

He was in a four-poster bed, flat on his back on a feather mattress. He was covered up to his chin with a thick crazy quilt and, he discovered after feeling himself, fully clothed.

"Disappointing," he muttered.

"There doesn't appear to be a concussion or fracture." Emily, wearing jeans and a ski sweater, her blond hair pulled back and tied with a strand of black ribbon, was sitting in a straight chair between him and the bedroom's small stone fireplace. "Fishbowl injuries, of course, can be—"

"Those references in my dossier to my occasional clumsiness are exaggerations," he informed her, sitting up. "Anyway, the most surefooted of operatives might slip during a torrential rainstorm. Especially if a wig unexpectedly—"

"What makes you think I've read your file, Trip?"

"Most pure-minded vicars' daughters I've met don't carry weapons concealed in their lingerie," he replied. "Who're you with?"

"Special Intelligence, same as you."

"No, that's an error. I'm retired," he said, reaching up to massage at a tender spot on his head. "For the past two years I've been peacefully teaching a course in Espionage Literature here at dear old Kingsley Academy. Not the most respected, or highest-paying, center of learning in our land. Yet sufficient for my humble—"

"The point is," she said, getting up to place another small log on the fire, "Special Intelligence does have a new assignment for you. Something the opposition apparently got wind of—"

"Even before I did. Pity, since had I been offered a job with SI, I'd have turned it down. Thereby saving the opposition the expense of outfitting a quintet of thugs in drag and sending them here to . . . who were they, by the way?"

"No identification on the dead and injured ones. We're checking it out," she answered. "The chap you were pursuing . . . um . . . got clean away."

Shedding the quilt, Seven attempted to swing out of bed. He found his legs a bit unreliable and settled for sitting on the edge. "What exactly is the job they think they're going to stick me with?"

"I have no details," Emily said. "Obviously, though, it's vastly important or—"

"Or they wouldn't have taken my name off the blacklist."

"I was going to say—or the other side, whoever they may be, wouldn't be striving to do you in."

"Men have sometimes been killed for trivial reasons, especially in the spy trade."

She steepled her fingers, rested her pretty chin on them. "That's almost certainly not the case this time," she assured him. "When you get up to London, you'll no doubt discover that—"

"I'm not going anywhere near London," he told her. "My career as one of Her Majesty's secret servants has long since ended. I intend to remain—"

"Surely, Trip, you don't intend to vegetate here in the wilds of Barsetshire for the rest of your life, lecturing to packs of scruffy boys on the brink of puberty about dull books by John Buchan, Dornford Yates, E. Phillips Oppenheim, and—"

"I do, yes. The quiet village life hereabouts appeals to me greatly."

"But you were an exceptional agent and—"

"Exceptional, be honest, Emily, in that I fouled up as many assignments as I—"

"But when you succeeded, you did so splendidly. That time, for instance, when you diverted the Nile and—"

"Luck," he said. "Chiefly luck."

"There's also the family tradition. Your father, after all, is James—"

"If we all had to follow in our fathers' footsteps, Emily, you'd wind up a vicar."

She laughed, rising and crossing to a sideboard. "I'm not actually the vicar's daughter."

"You fooled me. Proving yet again that I am not the crackerjack secret—"

"I'm a very convincing person." She picked up a tray upon which rested a bottle of Martell's brandy and two snifters. "Even keener men than you have been taken in by me."

He made a fresh attempt to stand. It was a shade more successful and he was able to get as far as the bedroom's other chair before giving in to an impulse to rest. ''When I finally do get here inside your bedroom, it turns out I'm in no shape to do much else but sit and chatter.''

''You're an excellent conversationalist.''

''That's not really the sort of testimonial one enjoys hearing in such surroundings.''

''Are you determined, then, to turn down the invitation to go to London?'' she asked him. ''There are several people at Special Intelligence who are quite anxious to talk with you, Trip.''

He started to shake his head, then realized his head still wasn't up to that. ''I intend to lie fallow for the foreseeable future.''

Resting the tray on the four-poster he'd vacated, Emily turned her back on him and poured two glasses of brandy. ''Hasn't it occurred to you that the opposition may not quit? Suppose they make another attempt to terminate you?'' Turning, she handed him a snifter. ''You might be killed, or at least seriously hurt. Some of the lads at Kingsley may be injured as well.''

''Some of the lads at Kingsley could do with a little assassination.''

''That's hardly the sort of attitude I expected you to—''

''The fellow you want to see is Mr. Chips. I understand he cherishes each and every pupil who—''

''Very well,'' she said resignedly, taking up the other glass. ''No hard feelings. Cheers.''

''Cheers.''

Their glasses clicked and each took a sip of their brandy.

Emily pulled her chair closer to his, sat. ''I hope, in the light of what's happened, that you and I shall continue to be chums.''

"Chums," he found himself mumbling. "Pals forever . . . bosom buddies . . ." He gripped the arms of the chair. "Damn . . . I'm a half-wit . . . you hoodwinked me again . . . doped my drink . . ." His backside rose a few inches from the chair cushion before he fell suddenly to sleep in midair and sat again.

"I told you I was very convincing." She caught the glass as it fell from his lax hand. "And I really do have to get you to London."

Chapter 3

LONDON

The balding man in the conservative gray business suit set down the thick file folder he'd been leafing through, sighed, and frowned across his sturdy wooden desk. "Am I losing perspective as I grow older," he inquired of the pudgy blond man in the sturdy leather armchair, "or are there more ninnies, twits, and nitwits in the world today than there were two or three decades ago?"

"Stands to reason there'd be more." The pudgy blond man was about forty, dressed in a conservative gray business suit. "Population is increasing by leaps and bounds. Therefore ninnies, twits, and nitwits will increase proportionately. Stands to reason, P, old fellow."

P sighed yet again. "There's another thing that's commencing to weigh me down," he said. "Special Intelligence's habit of tagging me with a letter. And P, of all letters. One might grow used to being . . . say, B.

And I've always fancied that X had a certain dash. But P."

"Consider how I feel, sir. They were out of letters by the time they got to me. Nothing particularly dashing about spending one's day as twenty-seven."

"Well," said P, glancing toward the shuttered windows of his dark-paneled office, "let's get back to this Triple 'O' Seven business." He picked up the folder. "I'd much prefer using his father."

Twenty-seven shrugged one plump shoulder. "James Blond, it's always seemed to me, has been vastly overrated," he said. "Granted the chap has a way with the ladies, and wears clothes well. But, dash it all, there's more to counterespionage than that. I've never agreed with him about martinis either. Unless you stir the—"

"Be that as it may, twenty-seven, I wish Blond were available now." He drew a sheet of thin blue paper from the folder. "He's very good with these situations where the fate of the Western World hangs in the balance."

"We aren't actually certain the fate of the Western World is hanging in the balance here, P," reminded 27, shifting in his chair. "Could be this Professor Schwefel is exaggerating. Fellow is, after all, an American, and they—"

"Not Ulrich Schwefel. He's a sound man." P tapped the folder. "He won the Meisjesachtig Prize in science in 'fifty-nine."

"Not familiar with that one. Important, is it?"

"The Meisjesachtig Prize gets little publicity, mostly because it's so beastly difficult to pronounce and—"

"Yes, I noticed you've pronounced it two different ways thus far."

"It is, however, a prestigious award and anyone who's won it must stand high in the scientific community."

"Schwefel is getting along in years, though. Could be the old boy's gone a bit dotty."

"He's still associated with the New Haven Biotech Institute," said P. "*They* must think highly of him, obviously. And during the war the fellow did some brilliant work."

"Which war?"

"Second World War, of course."

"Long time ago. Many a first-rate man has gone bonkers since then."

"Not Schwefel. Not the chap who invented Gas #104P."

Twenty-seven blinked. "Can't quite place that one. What's it do?"

P rubbed at his chin. "Matter of fact, its exact nature eludes me at the moment," he admitted. "I do know the stuff's highly thought of to this day. Pacifists are still agitating to get it banned."

Twenty-seven said, "I still don't see why this Professor Schwefel can't simply pass on his supposedly vital information to one of our other agents. We have several gifted fellows in America already."

"Schwefel can be annoyingly stubborn." P picked up a sheet of yellow paper. "He insists that he'll confide only in James Blond or to 'that curly-headed little boy of his.' "

"Obviously hasn't seen Triple 'O' Seven in a while. Not a little boy anymore," said 27. "Hair's not even particularly curly."

"Be that as it may, Twenty-seven, the professor will impart his information only to Blond or his son."

"Ask me, I'd wait until Blond is free."

"But that may not be for weeks." He held up a sheet of green paper. "Schwefel quite clearly implies that we must act quickly to avert a catastrophe of worldwide proportions."

"The trouble with Seven," said 27, "is that he's forever botching up assignments. Wasn't more than three years ago, out in Kabichiland, that he completely fouled up the assassination of King Skrubu."

"It was a difficult shoot," said P. "Quite windy at that ribbon-cutting ceremony for the new motorway across the veld."

"A difficult shoot mainly because Seven insisted on using a bow and arrow."

"He was in an emerging African nation, after all, and a bow and arrow seemed more approp—"

"Putting a poisoned arrow through the gizzard of Senator Rasmussen of Wisconsin, who was there representing the president of the United—"

"Rasmussen, according to the polls I've seen, wouldn't have won reelection anyway."

The plump agent said, "Very well, it appears we're stuck with Triple 'O' Seven and he with us. What did he say when you summoned him back to active service?"

P shut the folder. "He wasn't especially keen on it," he replied. "Initially he refused outright."

"Not something his father would do."

"You must keep in mind, though we don't like to dwell on the fact, that Seven had a Russian mother. She it was who stuck him with his rather unusual name."

"Russian humor tends to be ponderous," observed 27,

searching himself for his pipe. "Can one assume that Seven finally agreed to undertake this assignment?"

"We'll soon find out." P consulted his wristwatch. "He'll be arriving here shortly."

"Coming by train, is he?"

"Steamer trunk actually."

Twenty-seven filled his pipe. "Had to drug him?"

"Seemed the best way to get him here against his will."

"I much prefer to deal with a man who volunteers for a mission of this sort."

"He may volunteer yet," said P with hope.

Chapter 4

HAWAII

The green door flapped open and a naked, red-haired woman came sailing out into the bright afternoon. She described an arc across the warm air and landed on her bare backside amid the brush and flowery shrubs that bordered the lawn of the white gingerbread mansion.

The thickset Russian agent who'd been coming up the white gravel path swerved and went trotting over to her.

Disentangling herself from the foliage, the woman, who was about thirty-five, remarked, "They have a lousy retirement policy at this place."

"It's that way in my profession, too, Suzanne." He helped her to her feet.

The front door of the bordello swung open again. Two tan suitcases and a teddy bear were tossed out onto the lawn.

"You still haven't learned to relax, Ivan."

Ivan Turgenev had reached for the Brno CZ 83 automatic in his belt holster when the door started to move. "I was much calmer before they sent me here to Kidamona Island," he said, letting the gun slide back into the holster and going over to gather up her strewn luggage. "Perhaps you have something in here you can put on." Crouching, the KGB man opened one of the suitcases. "No, this seems to be nothing but black lace lingerie and manacles. And this other suitcase contains . . . um . . . whips and chains."

"Business equipment," said Suzanne. "I'll have to . . . Oh, here comes something more."

A plaid overcoat had come flapping out of the white Victorian bordello.

After helping Suzanne slip into the coat, Turgenev bowed politely and continued on his way to the front door of Mama Therese's establishment.

The front door opened again a few seconds before he reached it and a pair of high heel pumps were tossed out.

Dodging those, the KGB agent pushed inside.

A large Hawaiian in a white suit was standing in the foyer. "Want to help me fling the rest of her stuff out, Ivan?"

"I'm too sensitive for that sort of work." He went on into the parlor.

A fat, freckled man was sitting alone in there on a candy-striped love seat. He was sobbing quietly into a paper handkerchief. "I should've bought that pineapple plantation instead of this whorehouse," he said, sniffling and looking up at the Russian. "It always touches my soft Irish heart when one of the girls retires. 'Tis touched I am . . . Hey, Togo! Don't forget to toss her that bouquet . . . All the girls get a complimentary bouquet of roses upon leaving us. Well, it's actually azaleas in this instance because roses are too frapping expensive. The sentiment's the same, I say."

"I wish to see Mr. Jobb, Malley."

The proprietor blew his nose, destroying the handkerchief in the process. "Did you know I was once an altar boy in Dublin?"

"Yes, and you have a shamrock-shaped mole on your left—"

"That's right, you know everything. Fancy trying to keep anything from a Bolshie spy." Malley found another handkerchief in the lumpy pocket of his sport coat. "What I was leading up to was this—Old Father Kennedy would turn over in his grave were he to learn I was running a Hawaiian whorehouse under the name of Mama Therese."

"Father Kennedy is alive and therefore unable to turn over in his grave," said Turgenev, a bit impatiently. "He left the church in 1974, married a bareback rider, and emigrated to Iola, Wisconsin. You needn't, therefore, feel guilty. I wish to see Mr. Jobb."

Malley stood. "Thorough. You lads are thorough."

"Details are important, even small details."

"Bareback rider, was it? Yes, he was always fond of horses."

"Now, if you'd be so kind as to announce me to Mr. Jobb."

"Sure you wouldn't like to sample the wares, as it were, Mr. Turgenev? We have a fifteen-year-old virgin you might find . . . No, I take that back." He glanced at his gold wristwatch. "She's not back from school yet. But there's Miss Nancy, who's a virgin at heart if not—"

"I wish only to see Mr. Jobb."

Malley shuffled across the room. "Arrange yourself in that bentwood rocker if you will."

"Can't I simply descend by way of the stairs or—"

"Were it up to me, to be sure, I'd let you use the cellar stairs. But B.J. now, he's very high on all this secrecy and mumbo jumbo." The proprietor reached for a button on the pink-papered wall. "Hold on now, Mr. Turgenev." He poked the button.

The floor suddenly opened beneath the Russian and he and the chair dropped down into darkness.

The black man was large and there was a slightly Oriental cast to his features. He sat silently in the highback wicker chair at the center of the small, shadowy underground room, watching the newly arrived KGB man.

Getting to his feet, Turgenev dusted himself off. "General Bretsky is unhappy."

"It's the Russian soul," said Jobb.

"Perhaps. Let me say then that his unhappiness has been increased by recent events." Turgenev uprighted the chair that had fallen with him and sat in it. "You were supposed to have arranged for the death of Triple 'O' Seven."

Jobb leaned forward, causing his chair to creak and groan. "Bretsky has stuck me with a crew of . . . what might I call them? Um . . . assholes," he said. "Yes, assholes seems a fitting word." He held up a finger. "Not bad enough you people insist I work with an asshole who calls himself Dr. Yes." A second finger popped up. "On top of that, you stick me with an asshole who calls himself Dr. Maybe. And those two go and hire a gang of assholes who do all their work while dressed up in women's underwear and wigs and—"

"The general concedes that the Baroque Quintet was not an especially wise—"

"You stick me with a pair of fruitcakes who like to dress up like ladies. It stands to reason they'll have a tendency to hire other fruitcakes who like to dress up like ladies and—"

"Actually only Dr. Maybe has those tendencies," corrected Turgenev. "Dr. Yes is simply a cannibal on the side. But there's nothing odd about his manner of dress."

"That reminds me . . . he ate the Avon Lady." Jobb's dark face showed annoyance. "Cost me a lot to get that hushed up. Even had to buy all sorts of cosmetics and costume jewelry we don't need. Those extra costs'll be on the invoice I give you assholes when—"

"General Bretsky wants to know what you plan to do about the Triple 'O' Seven matter."

"I'm taking care of that on my own. I hired someone to do him in."

"Who?"

Jobb shook his head. "You don't need to know."

Turgenev snorted. "General Bretsky is also anxious to learn how the field tests on the . . . um . . . product are going."

"As well as can be expected."

"Which means?"

"Considering that I have mostly assholes working for me, we're rolling right along," Jobb told him. "We've been testing the stuff in places like East Moline, Illinois and Malaga, Spain. Seems to work just fine and we'll be ready for wider-scale tests any day now."

The Russian sat back in his chair, eying the other man. "You realize that General Bretsky contacted you initially, Mr. Jobb, because both your parents had had some connection with James Blond and—"

"Yeah, I understand that. He thinks it's amusing to put the sons of old Blond antagonists against Blond's son," said Jobb, frowning. "In my case that's smart, since I'm a first-rate espionage agent. But when you dig up assholes like Dr. Yes and Dr. Maybe, then you're going too—"

"They are, after all, the offspring of one of James Blond's most formidable foes and therefore—"

"You can't always count on heredity."

Turgenev rose. "General Bretsky will expect news of the death of Triple 'O' Seven in the very near future."

"He'll get it sooner than that," promised the black man.

Chapter 5

BRIDLEMERE, ENGLAND

The innkeeper wheezed, sighed, and deposited the heavy steamer trunk at the foot of the spool bed.

The trunk groaned.

"Thank you so much," said Emily Watts-Batsfree, who was clad in a smart traveling suit.

The bent old man touched his forelock. "Think nothing of it, muss," he said, wheezing again as he backed toward the doorway.

The trunk moaned.

Emily laughed suddenly. "Forgive me for teasing you," she said. "I'm a ventriloquist."

"Don't matter what your religion, muss, all are welcome at the Pegasus Inn." He resumed backing out of the cozy, beam-ceilinged room.

The trunk mumbled.

"No, I meant I was throwing my voice," explained the

blonde, pointing at the trunk. "Perhaps you've seen me on the telly."

"No, muss. I don't watch that much. Reception is right poor out here on these lonely moors. And I'm near deaf anyway." He nodded at the big trunk. "Was there some stunt you were wanting me to witness?"

"No, never mind."

The white-haired innkeeper reached out behind himself, catching hold of the brass doorknob. "Speaking of sounds now, muss," he said. "Pay no attention to any you may hear during the night. There's some as'll tell you the Pegasus Inn is haunted, but I can—"

"Haunted?"

" 'Tis nothing more than an old wives' tale. I've never heard a thing myself, muss," he assured her. "Nary a scream, or the telltale thump of a wooden leg upon the stair or the rattling of chains or the mournful cries of 'Parsifal, Parsifal, 'tis your long-lost love come back from the grave!' None of that have I heard, no."

Emily dropped her purse on the bureau. "One ghost does all that?"

"Nay, 'tis a group of them." He opened the room door. "The Pegasus Inn has stood here on this blighted ground since the reign of Arthur III, whenever that was, and there be those who swear the old place attracts assorted haunts."

"I won't let them bother me."

" 'Tis probable you'll not hear them at all on account of the fearsome storm."

"What storm?"

"There'll be a formidable one this night, muss." He rubbed at his left elbow. " 'Tis dusk now and I'd estimate the storm will hit within the hour. And shall I bring you a bit of supper up here to your—''

''No, thanks. Should I wish anything, I'll come down to the dining room.''

''Have a nice evening then, muss. Despite what you may hear, 'tis possible to enjoy yourself on this benighted moor.'' He touched his forelock again, backed out of the room, and shut the thick oaken door.

Emily bolted it on her side, turned, and walked to the trunk. ''If you promise to behave yourself, Trip, I'll let you out.''

''Ventriloquist, are you?'' said his voice, sounding a bit hollow. ''I was tempted to treat our boniface to a visit from the ghost of Triple 'O' Seven. Open up, will you?''

''In a minute. I have to find the key.'' She crossed to her purse. ''I know it's in here somewhere because I—''

''No need.'' The trunk lid raised with a creak and Seven, a bit rumpled, stepped free.

She gasped sedately. ''How on earth did you pick that lock from inside the—''

''I'm not a complete dolt, Emily.'' He brushed at the sleeve of his blazer. ''Who was the previous tenant of this trunk?''

She shrugged. ''I believe the vicar's cocker spaniel was fond of sleeping in it.''

''He invited in a few of his woodland friends, I imagine.'' He shook his head striving to clear it. ''I'm a bit disappointed that you drugged me, Emily. Well, actually, I'm a bit disappointed that I allowed you to do it. My father, from what I hear, was notably weak in that area himself and lovely lady spies were forever doping his martinis and—''

"Trip, I had to. SI simply must talk to you and—"

"Are they planning to drop in on us here at the Pegasus Inn—which is where, by the way?"

"Oh, it's near a town named Bridlemere. I'm not exactly sure just where that is. But in answer to your question, Trip, I hadn't intended to stop at all. But to barrel right on through to London."

"Not that I mind spending the night in a quaint country inn with you, but—"

"I could've left you and the trunk in the van for the night," she pointed out. "I calculated, though, that you'd be coming to soon and it seemed more humane to—"

"Explain to me why you halted for the night."

"It was the oddest thing," Emily said. "I all at once suffered two flat tires. They blew out just like that—*Pop! Pop*!—almost as though they'd been . . . Oh, Trip!"

"Been shot out?"

She nodded slowly, glancing toward the window.

At that instant a heavy metal shutter fell into place with a loud thunk.

And the door made a similar ominous sound.

Emily threw her arms around him. "Trip, a trap!"

He kissed her thoroughly, patted her buttocks, fondled her bosom. "Well, that's enough distractions," he said, pulling free of the pretty blond secret agent. "Now let's see about getting out of this pickle."

She smiled. "That's one of the things I find endearing about you," she said. "Your habit of calling the most horrendous dilemmas by quaint old-fashioned words such as pickle or jam or—"

"Is pickle no longer in fashion in intelligence circles?" He approached the door of the room.

Grabbing the antimacassar off the nearest armchair, he flung it against the door.

There was a sharp crackling sizzle when the fringed cloth hit the wood.

"Got the door electrified," he said, yanking a doily off the end table. This he lobbed into the shuttered window. "But not our window. Good."

The room—indeed, the whole inn, was commencing to make strange rumbling, grinding noises.

"Can this be the storm the spurious innkeeper predicted?" said Emily, watching Seven take a fat black fountain pen from his inner breast pocket.

"No, love, and it isn't spooks either."

As the rumbling increased, all the furniture took to jittering and swaying.

Seven dashed over to the window, aimed the point of the pen at the metal shutter.

A thin stream of smoking liquid shot out and started eating into the metal.

"Are you still using that old-fashioned fountain pen acid-gun?" asked Emily. "SI replaced those with ballpoint acid-guns over three—"

"Hush," he advised.

The room was shaking. The bed jumped three feet to the right.

Next came a deep, uneasy silence, followed by a brief sensation of weightlessness.

"The inn is living up to its name," remarked Seven.

"We're flying," realized Emily.

"Exactly. They've cleverly disguised a transport plane as a quaint country inn," he said. "We're now airborne."

"They anticipated that I'd be passing here, with you in a steamer trunk."

"That they did." He took a few steps back and then ran at the acid-soaked metal window shutter. He leapt and kicked at it with both feet.

He succeeded in booting the weakened metal clean out of the window, but got his right foot caught in the new opening and ended up dangling head down over the hassock.

"You always begin these things so splendidly," observed the young woman, aiding him in regaining an upright position.

He gave his head a shake, smoothed his mustache, and stared out the window. "Three thousand feet above the moor and climbing," he said, stepping up onto the hassock. "Wait here where it's safe, love."

"You're always saying things like that and then going out and getting yourself in a . . . um . . . pickle."

"I'm going to climb out and see if I can locate the cockpit of this craft."

Lightning crackled.

"The storm's starting up," murmured Emily. "Then the old coot wasn't a complete fraud."

"Could you give me a bit of a shove? I seem to be stuck in this window."

She obliged, fisting his backside. "There you go."

The night rain started just as he wriggled free of the window. He hung there on the side of the flying inn, supple fingers clutching the window frame.

Far below it was a deep blackness, with only a few faint dots of yellowish light. Directly under his feet a quaint wooden sign reading *Pegasus Inn—A Tradition Since the Days of King Arthur III* was flapping in the wind.

Seven took a few thoughtful deep breaths, nodded to himself, and started climbing up the outer wall of the inn.

"Do be careful," called Emily.

"Yes, I was intending too."

The ancient-looking crossbeams that fronted the inn facilitated his ascent. About ten rain-swept minutes later Seven pulled himself up onto the slanting shingle roof and clutched at the fat brick chimney.

"Five thousand feet up now," he guessed, glancing over the edge of the roof.

He shinnied up the chimney, took a look down into it.

There was light showing and he could make out a husky man in a flying suit sitting at the controls of the disguised flying ship. A bubble of plastic cockpit shield separated him from the control room.

Carefully he fished out another fountain pen. Grunting, he shinnied a bit higher and squirted the contents of the pen down into the chimney at the plastic.

He waited, counting slowly to twenty.

The wind was getting stronger, trying to tear him from the chimney.

". . . nineteen . . . twenty," he said at last.

He pulled himself over the lip of the chimney and dropped down it.

On the drop he picked up a considerable amount of soot.

When his feet hit the plastic it cracked and shattered, giving way.

Seven landed on his left hip right next to the nonplussed pilot.

Jumping to his feet, he yanked out his Beretta. ''Land this thing, old man,'' he ordered.

''Bloody hell!'' The pilot unbuckled, left his seat, took three skittering steps to his left, and dropped through a trap in the floor. ''Geronimo!'' came his voice a few seconds later.

Seven settled into the vacant seat. ''I suppose one can fly an inn about the same way one flies a regular plane,'' he said to himself as he took over the controls.

Chapter 6

LONDON

Seven, jaunty in conservative gray business suit and bowler hat, strolled into the outer office of Special Intelligence. He carried a rolled umbrella in his right hand, swinging it like a cane. "Top of the morning, Miss Manypiggies, you're looking . . . No, now I take a closer look, you appear to be decidedly under the weather," he said, stopping beside the desk. "Been ill, have you?"

"I'm not exactly Miss Manypiggies," confided the person behind the desk in a low, angry voice. "Actually, in point of fact, I'm Herbert Beerbohm Manypiggies, son of the original Miss Manypiggies."

Seven took a backward step. "I'm not especially keen on female impersonators at the—"

"Nor am I," admitted Herbert, patting his wig. "This is P's idea. The mater's off on a holiday and he thought it'd be jolly to have a second-generation Miss Manypiggies on duty."

"I'll speak to P and see if—"

"No, no," said Herbert. "If I don't hold down this job until the mater's back it'll be a black mark on my record. May even foul up my pension. Usually I'm with Clandestine Demolition and—"

"That is a fetching frock, though. And it looks very good on you," Seven pointed out. "So try to look on the bright side."

Herbert coughed into his hand. "We were expecting you to arrive in a trunk."

"As so often happens in this line of work, there's been a change of plans." He nodded at the far door. "I'm here of my own free will, anxious to undertake this new mission."

"Why wouldn't you be? So long as it doesn't involve wearing panty hose and . . . Well, no matter. Go on in, P's been awaiting your arrival."

P looked up as Seven entered his office. "How'd you get out of the steamer trunk?"

Grinning, he sat opposite his chief. "Before we get down to cases, P, let me pass this on to you." He extracted a folded sheet of yellow paper from his breast pocket, unfolded it, and handed it over to the chief of Special Intelligence.

"What's this? A bill for six hundred pounds for reseeding? Reseeding what?"

"The Bridlemere cricket field, sir."

P's eyes narrowed. "Why in heaven's name should we be paying for reseeding . . . but wait. It must have something to do with your not being delivered here by four-oh-six."

"Is that Emily's number? She never mentioned it."

"Well?" The bill fluttered in his grasp.

"When I landed the inn last evening, sir, I fear I ripped up the sod a bit," explained Seven, reaching into another pocket of his suit. "I don't know if you've ever tried to land an airship that had been disguised as a quaint country inn, especially during a severe rainstorm, but it's most assuredly tricky work. You'll want this one as well."

This bill was written on blue paper. "Seven hundred pounds for a bell tower?"

"St. Norbert's in the Field. I flew a bit too close." He grinned amiably, crossed his legs. "The bill for the sexton's leg won't be coming in for another few days. They're not even certain if it's a true break or only a—"

"Which sexton?"

"From St. Norbert's in the Field. Chap was up tuning the bells when I skimmed the tower."

P slumped slightly in his chair. "Is this all, Seven?"

"All but a few minor items, yes. There's only rental on the cottage, catering fees, and—"

"Cottage?" inquired P in a quiet voice.

"For Emily—that's four-oh-six to you—and I to spend last night in. There wasn't a room to be had at the only other inn in Bridlemere and so we had to rent the cottage. Very attractive little place, thatched roof, plaster lamb in the front yard," he said. "Rental was quite reasonable and we only had to sign a year's lease. The catering, in case you're curious, P, was for the little impromptu supper we gave for the constable, the vicar, the Bridlemere Boys

Choir—who were rehearsing in St. Norbert's at the time—and a Mrs. Whyte-Melville, who happened to be out walking her bulldog on the cricket field when I set down. Quite a jolly woman of mature years and one who added a good deal to the fun of the evening."

"I am not at this time," said P, slowly and carefully, "even going to ask how you came to be up in a flying inn."

"It's all in Emily's report, sir."

"And where might she be?"

"Still at the cottage. There was considerable tidying up to be done after the—"

"Four-oh-six was instructed to bring you here herself."

"No need for that. I came voluntarily."

P eyed the mustached secret agent. "Only a few days ago you refused to have any—"

"I happen to be angry now, sir," Seven replied. "There have now been two attempts on my life—and on Emily's, for that matter. While I would much prefer to continue my simple scholarly life in—"

"Good, good," cut in P. "No need to continue with your explanation. Go ahead and revenge yourself on these rascals. And do a good deed for Queen and country at the same time."

"Exactly."

"Let me then," said P, picking up a fat folder, "explain what's required of you, Seven."

After the briefing, P and Seven descended to the Special Weapons Section.

"Z has a few gadgets he'd like you to field test on this mission, Seven."

"Z? I don't believe I know the chap."

"He used to be U, but he was demoted," explained P. He stopped in front of a blank wall and passed his right hand across an electronic palm-print reader concealed therein. The wall made a small rumbling sound and part of it slid aside to reveal a doorway. "Someone in the PM's cabinet accidentally ate one of the chocolate bars into which Z had built a concealed . . . Ah, but here he is."

Z, his lab coat rumpled and his face even more wrinkled than it had been when last Seven had seen him, came shuffling across the large room to greet them.

The underground facility was very bright and housed long benches filled with electronic gadgetry and weapons. There were hundreds of guns of different sizes; motorbikes, cars, and what looked to be a flying saucer in a far corner.

"Just in time for the demonstration, gentlemen," said Z, smiling. "And, I must say, it's splendid to have you working with us once again, Seven."

"Thank you . . . um . . . Z, old man."

Z gestured at a king-size bed that had been set up on a clear patch of lab floor. "This appears, at first glance, to be nothing more than one of those adjustable beds so admired by our senior citizens. It conceals, however, a surprise or two," he told them. "Two thirty-two, will you step over here a moment?"

A heavyset woman in a yellow lab coat put down the candy bar she'd been tinkering with, grabbed a crash helmet off her worktable, and came over to them. "Now what?"

"Come, come, two thirty-two, that's hardly the attitude to exhibit in front of—"

"Let them be sodding guinea pigs for a bit," grumbled the woman as she strapped on the helmet. There was a bluish circle under her left eye and several bruises on her forehead. "Tries out all his flaming knicknacks on me, he does. Exploding breakfast cereal, bear-trap doormat . . ." She trailed off into a sigh.

"All I require you to do, two thirty-two, is stretch out on yon bed and relax."

"Relax, is it? How's a person to relax when she knows full well some new and devilish assault on her sensibilities is in the works?"

"And now to bed," urged Z.

Two thirty-two gave her helmet a pat, scowled, stomped over, and jumped atop the bed.

"I think this will surprise you." Z drew a small remote control unit from a cluttered pocket.

"Actually," said P, "you've pretty well taken away much of the element of surprise by having the lady don the protective helmet, Z. That, certainly, don't you know, tips your hand and alerts us that something dire is in the offing."

"Yes, yes, I suppose you're right," said Z forlornly. "I've tried to persuade her of that very thing, but she insists on the safety gear. And the union backs her up, alas." He punched a button on the control box.

Whang!

The upper half of the bed had snapped up and catapulted 232 clear across the wide room and into the far wall.

Thunk!

"Very impressive," commented P. "Now then, Z, if you'll fetch the weapons you've fashioned for Seven, we'll get on with—"

"She's not rising," mentioned Seven, staring across the room.

"Pay no attention," advised Z. "Two thirty-two likes to sham and pretend she's more seriously injured than she is."

"Nevertheless." He hurried through the maze of worktables and busy technicians to the place where the helmeted lady had landed. Crouching, he took hold of her wrist.

"Piss off," she whispered.

"Eh?"

"Begone, I'm shamming. Looks good on the report to the union . . . 'two thirty-two was out cold for nearly fifteen minutes.' "

"Yes, fine, I see." He stood up. "Appears she'll be unconscious for a bit, though it's nothing serious."

When he returned to Z's side, the scientist handed him a tiny container of what appeared to be breath spray. "This most certainly ought to come in handy."

"I find that proper flossing and brushing takes care of—"

"No, this actually contains a very powerful truth drug. One whiff causes your victim to speak nothing but the truth for up to five full minutes."

"I'll give it a try." Seven pocketed it.

"And here's something else you can carry around with you." He produced a roll of Life Savers, Tropical Fruit flavor. "Each of the candies is actually a powerful plastique bomb. I'd demonstrate, but since two thirty-two is still feigning—"

"No need, Z. I know how effective your miniature explosives can be." He placed the roll of candy in another of his pockets.

Z shuffled over to an attaché case that sat on a workbench next to an array of experimental stun guns. ''You'll never guess what's in here,'' he said, chuckling and starting to open it.

''Wait now,'' cautioned P. ''Oughtn't we to be wearing protective headgear before you—''

''Not at all.'' Chuckling again, Z opened the case, shook it, twisted a few knobs, and, in under sixty seconds, had a bicycle assembled and parked on the lab floor. ''A collapsible cycle, Triple. It is, you'll notice, a girl's style bike, but that proved to be much easier to fold up.''

Seven was examining it. ''Only three-speed?''

''Thus far, yes. Although I anticipate having a ten-speed ready by this time next month.'' Deftly Z folded it up into its case. He held the case out to Seven.

''Actually, old man, I don't think I'll be needing a bicycle on this particular—''

''Take it anyway,'' suggested Z. ''No telling when you'll be in a tight corner—and a bicycle, even a three-speed girl's bike, may be just the thing you need.''

After hesitating a few seconds, Seven accepted the attaché case. ''Is that the lot then?''

''It is, unless you want one of these beds.''

''I think not.''

Chapter 7

NEW HAVEN, CONNECTICUT

Actually, Professor Ulrich Schwefel's sandstone mansion was sixteen miles to the south of New Haven and sat on a low bluff above the waters of the Long Island Sound. Triple 'O' Seven arrived there at a few minutes past eleven on a sunny Tuesday morning. He was driving a rented 1978 Datsun.

He turned on to the white gravel drive that cut across the vast, steeply slanting lawn and drove around to the three-car garage. After parking near a red truck that had *Shichi-Shi Bros.—Lawn Services* lettered on its doors, Seven opened the door and eased out of the car. He was carrying his attaché case in his left hand.

He noted that the door handle had come off in his right hand. "P and his budget cuts," he muttered, dropping the handle into the pocket of his blazer.

A large man was working on the hedges next to the red brick porch of Professor Schwefel's home.

Seven paused on the first step, frowning toward the gardener. "I say," he called to him, "am I mistaken or are you wearing the distinctive black and crimson robes of one of Japan's most vicious and dedicated secret orders of assassins?"

The huge Japanese turned to scrutinize him. "Allow me to put forth a counter question," he said politely. "Are you Triple 'O' Seven?"

"I am, yes," he answered. "I notice you're cropping the professor's hedge with a sixteenth century ceremonial Japanese killer sword."

"Actually I've been awaiting your advent, Mr. Seven." With a fierce cry, robes billowing, he came charging at him.

Nimbly dodging the charge and the deadly swish of the sword, Seven swung out with his attaché case.

"Oof," remarked the Japanese killer as the case connected with his crotch.

Rattle!

The case popped open and started converting into a three-speed girl's bicycle.

The seat went sliding under the shrieking assassin's backside and the newly assembled bike rolled backward down and across the sharply sloping lawn.

"Death to Triple 'O' Seven!" the Japanese cried, chopping at the air with his big sword and struggling to disentangle himself from the swiftly careening cycle.

The bike reached the edge of the grounds, bounced twice, and then went sailing over the edge toward the sea some three hundred feet below.

"Pity," said Seven, shaking his head. "Z intended me to test that bike more thoroughly than this."

From below came the distinctive sound produced when a three-speed bicycle and a dedicated Japanese assassin hit a rocky shore.

Drawing his Baretta, Seven climbed up to the front door.

He noticed now that the oaken door was an inch or so open.

Booting it fully open, he jumped to the side.

Only silence came out of the house at him.

After counting slowly to fifty, Seven dived across the threshold, gun held in both hands.

He found himself in a long, tiled hallway.

At its far end was a large, bright, glass-walled living room.

In the center of a white carpet lay a beautiful, auburn-haired young woman. She was completely naked, except for the twists of yellow rope that bound her.

"There," said Seven, removing the gag from the naked young woman's mouth.

"Oh, thank you," she said.

"Glad to be of service." He went to work on the ropes that tied her wrists behind her slim, tanned back. "My name is Triple 'O' Seven."

"Yes, I imagined that's who you were. Pleased to meet you. I'm Tilda Schwefel. My father sent me over to meet you, but I'm afraid that Japanese assassin got the jump on me."

Seven was frowning at a small tag that was attached to the length of rope. It said *Property of the George Jessel Theatre, Manhattan*. "Isn't your father here?"

"No, he was called away unexpectedly to an important conference on the Politics of Irrigation," Tilda replied, flexing her freed hands. "He instructed me to meet you here and drive you over to the campus to await his return."

Seven went to work on the ropes around her trim ankles. "He wasn't much good at knots."

"Well, I imagine when you specialize in chopping people to bits with a big ceremonial sword you tend to neglect learning things like tying knots and—"

"I'll get you something to put on— Why, might I ask, are you unclothed? Did that chap attempt to—"

"Oh, no, he was very polite—for a crazed assassin," said Tilda, standing up with his assistance. "It's simply that he caught me as I was stepping out of the shower."

Nodding, Seven started across the room toward a closet door. "Perhaps there's something in here to put on," he said, opening the closet and peering in. "Might I ask you a somewhat personal question, Miss Schwefel?"

"It's the least I can do, since you've just saved my life."

"Have you had any cosmetic surgery done on any part of your body lately?"

"Why, no. I must say, that's an odd inquiry."

Seven, his back to her, reached for the Baretta he'd reholstered. "The art of impersonation is more challenging than some realize," he said, the gun back in his hand. "You probably weren't aware that the true Tilda has a distinctive birthmark—in the shape of a skewed asterisk—on her left buttock. I wouldn't have known that myself had my chief not insisted that I memorize the dossiers of all the persons invol—"

Kachow!

A slug from an Iver Johnson Trailsman pistol dug into the wall some three inches to the left of his head.

Dropping and whirling, he fired at the naked young woman.

She was in the act of jumping behind a low black sofa on the other side of the room. She held a gun in her right hand now.

Seven rolled across the carpet, stood, and leapt for a flat white armchair.

"Ow!"

He'd banged his hand on the chair back in mid-leap; his Baretta was knocked free of his grasp and went bouncing away across the rug and out of reach.

"You're a bit brighter than I expected," called the false Tilda, sending a shot in the direction of his new hiding place. "I slipped up on that damn birthmark."

"You people tend to confuse me with my father," he said from behind the fat chair. "I'm not as easily distracted by the undraped female form as he is rumored to be."

"Yes, I did assume that if I stripped down to my skin it would put you off your guard."

"Don't imagine that I don't appreciate a young lady built as splendidly as you are," he called. "It's just that I put duty—as well as self-preservation—first."

"Speaking of which," she said from behind the sofa, "I still have my weapon, whereas yours is out here on the rug next to a spilled bowl of party mix. What say you surrender, Seven, and come out. We can talk over—"

"Come now, dear lady. You don't intend to negotiate with me," he pointed out. "Your late colleague had death in mind for me. You, I presume, were planted in here to do away with me should he fail."

After a few seconds she answered, "Well, yes, that's true. But since it really doesn't look like you're going to get out of this, Seven, why not just let me kill you and get it over with. I do have a lunch date in Westport at one and I still have to dress."

From his blazer pocket Seven took the special roll of Life Savers. "Tilda?"

"Yes?"

"I have here a very powerful new explosive," he told her. "What I intend to do is give you sixty seconds to clear out. If you don't I'll toss it into your hiding place."

"You're bluffing."

"No, I never bluff," he assured her, unwrapping the roll of candy and, carefully, extracting the topmost Life Saver. "I hate to cause a lady who's built along your lines to be blown to smithereens. Yet you give me no choice."

"Bluff," she reiterated.

Sighing, Seven began counting to sixty aloud. When he'd concluded, he said, "Ready to surrender, Tilda?"

"Nope."

He sighed again and threw the Life Saver over the top of his chair and toward her sofa.

Click!

It hit the coffee table, rolled across that, and dropped to the carpeting.

Nothing further occurred.

Chapter 8

Tilda said, "Okay, can we knock off the fooling around?"

Seven had noticed a tiny slip of paper rolled up with his Life Savers. "Half a moment, love."

Important! read the slip. *In order to detonate this candy, be sure to pull the pin*.

"The pin?" he said under his breath.

He peeled a second Tropical Fruit Life Saver, brought it up close to his narrowed eyes. There was a tiny pin visible.

"Now it's my turn to count to sixty," said Tilda. "Then I'm coming after you, shooting."

"I caution you against it," he warned. "I've got this figured out now, and it's going to knock you flat."

"Hooey," she observed. "One-two-three . . ."

It took him three tries to get hold of the triggering-pin and get it tugged free of the tiny Life Saver. "That does it," he said finally, grinning grimly. "Hit the deck!"

He tossed the second Life Saver in her direction and hunkered down into a fetal position.

Approximately six seconds passed.

Kaboom!

Kablam!

There was a great deal of cracking, smashing, tinkling. The big view window was blown completely free of its frame.

Furniture thumped, banged, and whomped.

The chair he was behind was slammed hard into him.

A considerable amount of acrid smoke blossomed in the living room.

Seven put the rest of the candy away in his coat pocket. He very slowly and carefully started crawling out from behind the chair.

The sofa that the enemy agent had been using as a shield was no longer in the room.

Neither was the false Tilda herself.

Seven stood up, coughing as the swirling smoke got into his lungs. He retrieved his pistol from amid the remains of the glass and metal coffee table, and made his way over to where the window had been.

There was a patio out beyond that and then a steep drop down to the Sound.

What had been the arm of the black sofa was twisted around a low iron railing at the far side of the patio.

"A shame," said Seven. "She was a very attractive young woman, and under other circumstances we might have hit it off."

From down on the water came the sound of a motorboat starting up.

Seven ran to the edge and looked down just in time to see a black launch roar away across the blue midday water. He had the impression that there was a naked woman at the controls.

"Vot's der dodgosted meanink of dis?" demanded an angry voice behind him.

Seven pivoted, gun in hand. "Professor Schwefel, isn't it?"

"Who elz vould be hoppink around mine ruined livink room?" A thickset man of sixty stood at the edge of the patio, glaring out at him. His hands were free, but his ankles were still tied with yellow rope. "I hope you dodgosted sigrid agents got insurance."

The angry professor shooed Seven off, bent, grunted, and untied his ankles. "Better dan Houdini I vas," he said. "Anudder fife minutes und I'd have been free. Den I vould've captured all dese bummers mithout ruinink mine—"

"Where's your daughter?"

"Tilda? Shacked up mit dot no good lowlife fogsinger out in Peoria. Same like always."

"The young lady who tried to terminate me was posing as your daughter. So I was naturally concerned as to the whereabouts of the actual—"

"Did she stood around mit her mouth half open all der time? Did she try to convince you dot a lowlife vot sinks about clean air—did Wagner ever write about clean air? —is better dan a feller vot works for a livink? If she done dot, den she vas impersonatink mine dumgoozled daughter."

Seven came back inside the ruined living room. "If you have a vacuum cleaner, sir, I might be able to lend a hand in cleaning up this—"

"I chust now recognized dot curly hair," the husky professor said. "You is got to be liddle Tribble 'O' Sevunt."

"I am, yes. We met many years ago when I was a lad at—"

"You ain't pigged up much smartness offer der years, mine boy." Professor Schwefel crunched across the debris and out into the tiled hall. "A simple bop on der coco vould've incapacitated dot bimbo. Instead you destroy half mine—"

"I'm not in the habit of hitting women, sir."

"Hah! You neffer had a daughter like mine Tilda."

Seven cleared his throat. "You were anxious to see me, sir. Perhaps we—"

"I vouldn't haff been zo anxious if I'd known you vas gunner blitzkrieg mine abode und dumb mine furniture in der drink."

"Obviously it's important to the KGB to keep us from getting together. So we better start talking about what's worrying you, sir."

"Vot's afoot, Tribble, is dis," said the professor, opening the front door and stepping out into the sunshine. "One of mine colleagues has defected to der udder side and is helpink dem cook up sometink vot'll incapacitate about ninety percent uff der dodgosted free vorld."

Chapter 9

Professor Schwefel prowled his paneled den as he talked. "Dis colleague uff mine is Dickens Underfoot, a dod-gosted boy genius."

"How old is he?"

"Forty siggs."

"Bit long in the tooth to be classified a boy genius."

"Vell, Dickens has been a boy genius since he vas fourteen. I guess I chust keep thinkink uff him dot vay."

"Would you have some pictures of him?"

"Chust vun." Halting in front of a wall of bookshelves, Schwefel pulled out a thick volume. "Dis is his college yearbook." He thumbed through the pages. "Yah, here he vas."

Seven accepted the open yearbook, set it across his knees, and studied the photo the professor was pointing to. "Has an exceptionally prominent nose, doesn't he?"

"Dot's because dis is a picture uff him playing der starring part in *Cyrano de Bergerac*. It's der only picture I got."

"Yes, I see. Makes it a bit difficult to determine what he looks like at the moment."

"At der moment his nose ain't so big." The professor took the yearbook and replaced it on the shelf.

"What exactly has this Underfoot chap discovered that's so dangerous, sir?"

Professor Schwefel sat behind his cluttered desk. "It's somthink vot could screw up Vestern civilization as ve know it."

"One of those things, eh?" said Seven, nodding. "Can you give me more specifics?"

"Vell, uff course. Dot's vhy I sent for you . . ." He drummed his thick fingers on a clear patch of desktop. "Vell, actually I sent for your papa first, but dose dodrotted ninnies in Special Intelligence claimed he vas on a hush-hush assignment und couldn't come." The professor gave a resigned shrug. "So I settle for you, Tribble."

"I appreciate your confidence, sir. Though I'm wondering why you didn't try your own CIA or—"

"Ach, dose dumbbells. Dem I don't trust," he said. "Although I got to admit dey neffer blew up mine livink room."

Seven said, "Can you explain Underfoot's invention to me?"

From the clutter atop his desk Schwefel gathered up a handful of newspaper clippings. "Probably you didn't notice dis a couple veeks ago." He passed a clipping to him.

"From one of those scandal sheets, isn't it? I seldom peruse such—"

"Chust read der dodgoozled think."

" 'Spaniards Take Sexy Siestas.' Typical tabloid headline," he observed, skimming the story. "Upshot seems to be that an increasing number of the denizens of Malaga, Spain, are spending their time in amorous pursuits. This has resulted in business dropping off, the local government going to pot, and the tourist trade suffering a bit." He rested the newspaper cutting on his knee. "Having spent considerable time in Spain, I don't find it ominous that they're jumping into bed with each other. They're an—"

"How about East Moline, Illinois? Or Youngstown, Ohio?"

"Not as fiery as Malaga, I don't suppose."

"Yet I got clippinks, und some computer printouts, vot indicates similar stuff has been goink on dere, too." He shook his fistful of clippings and memos.

"You mean there's been increased sexual activity in those spots as well, Professor?"

"Yes, und we're in for serious trouble."

"Explain if you will."

"Dickens Underfoot was working under a grant from a large cosmetics firm," began the professor. "His assignment was to come up mit a new perfume, vun dot vould make any lady vot used it dodgosted irresistible."

"I'm surprised that an academic institution of the standing of yours would stoop to taking money from commercial—"

"Look, ve ain't got a football team. So ve got to hustle der business vorld," he said. "Anyvay, Underfoot came up mit somthink much too powerful for der perfume business. You should've seen vot it done to der lab mice. Dis stuff uff his causes whoeffer gets a viff to become obsessed mit makink luff und similar hankypanky. Und vun dose lasts for veeks."

Seven smoothed his mustache thoughtfully. "And you believe that's what's causing these apparent outbreaks of amorousness in Spain and Ohio and elsewhere?"

"Absolutely. Underfoot skipped out vun mongth ago und der first outbreak vas a veek later," said Professor Schwefel. "Dose chumps at der school tink he's on a sabbatical in Hawaii, but I know bedder." Schwefel's hands turned to fists. "I'm sure Dickens Underfoot vas recruited by foreign agents who got vind uff his invention."

"How's the stuff delivered—how do you administer a dose?"

"It's a spray. I don't know how he's applying it in der field. Obviously not mit der little atomizers he used on der mice."

"You're afraid the use of Underfoot's invention will spread?"

"Uff course. Right now I suspect dey're fieldtestink der stuff, to make sure it vorks on human beinks," said the professor. "If dey use der stuff on sufficient people, den our society vill collapse. Nobody vill bother to go to vork, nobody vill care about amassing vordly goods or fighting der vay up der ladder of success."

"Sounds pretty horrible all right." Seven frowned. "Is there any antidote?"

"Not yet. Although I am vorking on one," said Schwefel. "Und I tell you vhy—dere's somethink Underfoot may not know about his invention."

"Which is?"

"After he defected, und about sixty days after he'd tried the latest version uff der stuff on der mice—der mice started dying."

Chapter 10

NEW YORK CITY

The pale yellow-haired young man seated at the white grand piano was unhappy. "I ain't chipper, ducks," he informed the pretty auburn-haired young woman seated across the sun-bright penthouse living room. "I ain't bubbling over with good feelings, Kate."

Kate Smithsonian shrugged her left shoulder. "That's the way things go in espionage, Alfie."

Alfred Hawkshaw struck a few discordant chords. "Who's talking about espionage," he said. "What I'm ticked off about is that these sods won't let Belphoebe repeat her London role in my musical. What I mean is, she was brilliant as Esmeralda in my musical version of *The Hunchback of Notre Dame* over there. Nobody can handle a tambourine like my dear wife, but now they claim they have to have an American actress play the part in the

American opening." He whapped the keyboard a few more times. "Not bloody likely. I'll shut the whole show down before I—"

"As I understand it, Alfie, the producers have built a full-scale replica of Notre Dame cathedral on the stage of the George Jessel Theatre on Broadway."

"So?" Hawkshaw left the white piano bench, commenced pacing the black carpet.

"They might feel, since they've got a considerable amount invested—"

"I'm talking about art, ducks."

Kate said, "What I actually dropped in to chat about was our espionage assignment."

Striding over to the one vast window, Hawkshaw glared out. "Twits," he said to the view.

"I failed to eliminate Triple 'O' Seven," she said. "Also didn't silence Professor Schwefel."

"I mean to say, the London *Times* said they'd never seen anybody handle a tambourine like Belphoebe. 'Best impersonation of a spirited Gypsy girl these old eyes have feasted on in many a moon,' is how *Punch* put it. Now these sods tell us that—"

"Alfie, you're paid by B.J. to carry out certain—"

"And it isn't that I'm married to Belphoebe. I mean, I had two wives prior and I never tried to force them into any of my other musicals, did I now? No, you didn't see me shove Elana into my musical version of *Johnson's Dictionary*."

"I'm not a real theater buff. What we have to—"

"I certainly didn't insist that they star my second wife, Ziggy, in the American run of my musical adaption of

Remembrance of Things Past. No, even though she'd played Odette brilliantly in the West End. All in all, I've been a prince of—''

''Triple 'O' Seven is still alive. By now Professor Schwefel has informed him about the Underfoot Formula.''

''The goat we've hired for the American production adores Belphoebe, too. What I mean is, you stick some American bird in there as Esmeralda and it's going to upset the goat.'' He thrust his fists into the pockets of his white designer jeans. ''What were you nattering about, ducks?''

''I've been trying to remind you, Alfie, that you're a secret agent,'' Kate said. ''This musical writing business is only a cover for the real work you do. So I think—''

''My true career is music.'' He tapped himself on his narrow chest. ''Maybe at first it was a cover, but after my musical version of *Moby Dick* opened in London six years ago, I knew what my real calling was, ducks. 'Telling the story from the point of view of the whale and giving him all the best songs is a brilliant bit of dramaturgy.' That's what the blinking *Times* had to say. True, too.''

''Alfie, B.J. is going to be extremely upset about this, especially since he's working for the KGB in this instance,'' said Kate. ''Granted, it was mostly my fault the two of them survived. Still, you're in charge of this particular—''

''Kate, there's no need to fret and worry.'' Hawkshaw returned to the piano bench. ''We'll have another go at this Seven bloke. Women are his weakness, aren't they?''

''I'm not sure. Seeing me naked didn't distract him all that much.''

Hawkshaw nodded. "Well, Kate, it's possible you simply lack star quality," he told her. "Belphoebe has it. Even partially clothed she can attract—"

"You have a new plan?"

"Certainly. I'm going to tell them I'll cancel the American premier unless they use—"

"A plan to terminate Seven."

"Not at the moment," admitted Hawkshaw. "Perhaps you and I had better come up with one."

The banjo player had about fifty dollars in paper money stuffed into the tin cup that sat on the sidewalk next to his tapping foot. He was a lean man of forty-one, sitting on a weathered canvas chair in front of the Showbiz Deli on Broadway.

Triple 'O' Seven paused, deposited two quarters in the cup. "eighteen-fifteen-fourteen," he said. "Seven-fifteen-twenty-two-twelve-one-eighteen-twenty."

"I might've known." The lean man ceased his strumming, rested his banjo across his narrow lap. "Everybody has been dropping dollar bills or better, but leave it to a Special Intelligence agent to—"

"I'm anxious to contact our local—"

"Do you know what I've taken in so far today—and it isn't even three in the afternoon yet?" He grabbed up the cup, dug out the money and put it into the frayed pocket of his rumpled sport coat. "Nearly two hundred dollars. Now you figure if I could do this five days a week, that'd bring in a thousand a week. That's an income of fifty thousand a year, and tax free. Ten years and you'd have a half million, which if invested in government bonds or—"

"I want to see our chief local agent."

"And I only know seventeen tunes on the banjo. Doesn't seem to matter."

Seven grinned, leaned, and rested a hand on the neck of the banjo. "Unless you want me to whap you on the noggin with this, old man, I suggest you tell me how to make the contact."

"Just go into this delicatessen and sit in Booth 4," instructed the undercover agent. "When the waitress asks for your order, repeat the number sequence you just gave me. If you have time, you might try the Nova Scotia salmon on a hard roll. It's really quite—"

"Thanks." He contributed two more quarters to the cup and headed on into the Showbiz Deli.

He strolled by booths 1, 2, and 3.

Booth 4 was occupied by a plump old man—who seemed to be asleep with his face in his plate of corned beef and boiled potatoes—and a dark-haired teenage girl who was maybe ten pounds underweight.

She blushed up at Seven. "This is very embarrassing."

"How so, my dear?"

"Well, I'm trying to figure out whether or not Uncle Eli's had one of his seizures."

"Has them often, does he?"

"Fairly often, but he also passes out quite a bit from too much cheap wine. And if that's the case, he'll yell at me if I call an ambulance."

Seven smiled amiably, sliding in next to Uncle Eli. He took hold of the unconscious man's wrist. "Pulse seems quite regular."

"Then he's probably just drunk, wouldn't you think?"

Sniffing, Seven said, "That appears to be it. Would you like me to help you get him to a taxicab?"

"That'd make him mad, too. He should sleep it off in a while."

"I'll sit here for a moment or two, to be sure all's well."

"That'll be nice," she said, sighing. "This whole thing isn't going at all well, you know. See, I have a weight problem sort of and Uncle Eli brings me here a couple times a week to fatten me up."

Seven studied her. "Slender young women are very much in vogue at the moment."

"Well, that's not what Uncle Eli thinks. I had to eat three bagels and two bowls of rice pudding today. But when he passes out, I get so nervous I can't eat again for a day or so," she explained. "We're not making any progress."

"You going to order anything, sir?" inquired the plump, gray-haired waitress who'd appeared beside the booth.

"Eighteen-fifteen-fourteen," said Seven. "Seven-fifteen-twenty-two-twelve-one-eighteen-twenty."

"Oy, that's an awful big order," the waitress remarked. "Eighteen is your brisket sandwich and fifteen's the roast beef, which means you're getting two sandwiches and on top of that chicken soup, carrot cake, cheese blintzes, and—"

"Is this your regular booth?" He stood.

"Well, not exactly, no. It's Bev's, except she's taking a break in the ladies and I'm filling in."

"I'd best wait for her."

"Is there something wrong with my service, sir? I've been on duty here, rain and shine, for sixteen and a half years next Tuesday and nobody's ever—"

"I'd better confess that this is an affair of the heart."

"Does her husband know?"

"I fear he's just found out. While he was reaching for the shotgun, I fled over here to warn her."

"There's no telling about romance," said the waitress, shaking her head. "Here Bev's thirty pounds heavier than me and she's got a cutie like you on the string. How can you figure that?"

"Perhaps you'd better fetch her."

"Sure, you wait right here."

The thin teenager asked, "Are you really her secret lover?"

"Not exactly," he admitted. "But the truth is much too complicated to go into."

"That's what Uncle Eli always says. You and he share that philosophy," she said. "He lies quite a lot."

"Psst," came a voice. "This way." An even chubbier waitress was beckoning to him from the aisle.

Chapter 11

The Special Intelligence agent apologized again for his mittens and had another go at the computer terminal keyboard on his small metal desk. "This office is only temporary," he said for the second time.

"Rather clever actually, Y," said Seven, who was perched on a barrel of pickles, "using the pantry of a delicatessen as your headquarters."

"Too bloody cold they keep it," complained Y, adjusting his woolen scarf and then squinting at the display screen. "Actually, we were supposed to be hidden in the basement of a boutique three blocks from here and nearer Lincoln Center, but six-twelve signed the wrong lease."

"Don't believe I know the chap."

"Used to be W, but he was demoted after this business."

"Anything about the young lady who had a go at killing me?"

Y rubbed the frost off the screen with the heel of his mittened hand. "Going by your description, Seven—which was commendably detailed, by the way—you did say those freckles were more pronounced on the left breast than on the right, didn't you?"

"Left breast, yes."

"Then there's no doubt on the identification. Yes, her name is Kate Smithsonian. She's twenty-eight, a native of New Zealand."

"Who's she working for?"

"She's a free lance, usually employed by the other side."

"Can you be a bit more specific?"

"KGB most often, but also for a variety of crazed master criminals bent on world domination."

"Sounds like she's a bit of an idealist."

"She's belonged to a great many peace organizations, marched against the bomb in six separate countries, and she subscribes to a dozen extremely liberal magazines."

"Didn't realize there were that many," remarked Seven, shifting his position on the pickle barrel.

"This girl looks to be a dangerous radical, Seven," said Y, scowling.

Seven asked, "Any notion whom she's employed by at the present moment?"

"Computer thinks it's KGB once again," replied Y after rubbing the display screen once again. "But possibly not directly. We hear there may be a chap known as B.J. in the woodpile."

"Does this B.J. tie in directly with what I'm working on?"

"Don't know as yet. Suggest you keep your eyes and ears open."

Nodding, Seven next inquired, "What have you got on this missing Dr. Underfoot?"

After buttoning up the topmost button of his overcoat, Y addressed the keyboard. "Ah, here it is," he said, pausing to shiver. "Subscribes to all the same radical magazines as that Kate Smithsonian girl."

"Anything besides that, sir?"

"He was last seen in Honolulu three weeks ago. Left his hotel without checking out. Not seen since."

"What about this gas or mist—the stuff Professor Schwefel told me about?"

"Nothing. We apparently weren't aware of the true nature of Underfoot's work, nor that it posed a threat to civilization as we know it."

Seven stood, rubbing his hands together. "Who owns the George Jessel Theatre?"

"Is this pertinent, or have you decided to play show business trivia?"

"It pertains, sir."

Y consulted the computer. "Jove," he said after a few seconds, "that's interesting."

"What?"

"The George Jessel's owned by a conglomerate based in West Germany. The Langweilg Corporation—a company we've long had under scrutiny. We suspect they have links with the Russians. Why did you ask about this theater?"

"Had a hunch someone associated with the place took part in the assault on the professor," replied Seven. "The ropes used to tie him, and those the Smithsonian lass trussed herself up in, came from there.'' He began a little running in place to keep warm. ''I believe I'll drop in at the theater this evening.''

''Nothing is playing there just now. Place's being renovated for *The Hunchback of Notre Dame*. Dreadful musical, saw it in London. Wife insisted. She loved it.''

Seven's breath was coming out white. ''I'll be getting along, sir.''

''Don't blame you,'' said Y. ''Keep on guard. This situation's where the fate of the Western World is at stake can get a bit dangerous.''

Seven didn't answer his hotel room phone until the eleventh ring. ''Yes?'' he said, just a shade breathlessly.

''About to give up on you,'' came Y's voice. ''You took a deuced long time in answering.''

''Sorry, sir. I was throwing the maid out the window.''

Y asked, ''Any special reason?''

''Turned out to be a secret agent chap in disguise.''

Y made a disapproving sound. ''Good deal too much of this transvestism going about to suit me.''

''This fellow attempted to knife me while I was dressing for dinner.''

''What floor are you on?''

''Fifteenth.''

''Then there won't be any opportunity to question this latest assassin.''

''Afraid not, no.''

''Can't be helped,'' said Y. ''You'd best move into another hotel.''

"Intend to."

"Well then, now to the purpose of my call," said Y, sounding forlorn. "I'm afraid, Seven, that the CIA has put its oar in."

"In what way?"

"I've been instructed by P that we must henceforth cooperate with Central Intelligence on this Underfoot matter. How they got wind of it I don't know."

"I'd rather not. American agents tend to—"

"There's no avoiding it. We have our orders."

"How am I to cooperate?"

"To start off, you're to rendezvous with a CIA agent at midnight tonight."

"Where?"

Y gave the address of a town house on the fashionable East Side of Manhattan.

"Must say these CIA blokes go first cabin. No huddling in a meat locker for them," said Seven. "What's the name of my contact?"

Y hesitated. "I do hope I took this down correctly. His name seems to be Bubber Kapusky. Can that be right?"

"Noted American footballer of a decade ago, I think," said Seven.

"Never been interested in sport," said Y. "Wife dotes on it. Report to me as soon as you've met with him."

"I will, sir."

"Bubber," muttered Y and hung up.

Chapter 12

HAWAII

B. Jobb hopped from his wicker chair, pointing at the pudgy Oriental who was reclining on the wicker sofa. "What's that you're nibbling on, Dr. Yes?"

"Colonel Sanders."

"Didn't I tell you not to eat people in my—"

"It's fried chicken," said the leaner Oriental who occupied the wicker love seat in B.J.'s underground lair. "Stop teasing him, Yes."

Snickering, Dr. Yes tossed a bone over his shoulder. "For a man who lives down under a cathouse, B.J., you certainly are critical of other people's foibles."

"Cannibalism is a bit more than a foible." Slowly, the large black man settled back into his chair. "Did you, by the way, do anything to a lady who was in the neighborhood yesterday selling garden seeds? She's missing."

Dr. Yes licked his lips. "I was fasting yesterday. Wasn't I, Maybe?"

Dr. Maybe gave a confirming nod. "He's trying to shed a few pounds. That's tough for him because of the high fat content of human—"

"Spare me the cannibal diet tips," rumbled B.J. "Let's get back to business."

"Life's no fun if it's all business," Dr. Yes told him. "You have to stop and smell the roses."

"Smell all the damn roses you want. Just quit eating the neighbors."

Dr. Yes held up two pudgy fingers. "A couple of them is all, B.J."

Snatching up a sheaf of papers from atop the wicker coffee table, B.J. said, "I'm no longer satisfied with this lady agent of ours—Kate Smithsonian."

"Too skinny," said Dr. Yes.

"I give you a whole list of simply wonderful alternative ladies, B.J.," said Dr. Maybe. "It really does seem to me, you know, that in these international intrigue affairs one needs a female with a much more snappy and flamboyant name than Kate Smithsonian."

"Kate Smith," said Dr. Yes, snapping his plump fingers. "Didn't there used to be a lady singer named that?"

"That has nothing to do with—"

"Yes, Kate Smith was her name. Big fat lady singer. There was a meal for you."

Dr. Maybe wiped at his saffron forehead with a silken handkerchief. "I'm certain every lady on that list will do a better job than Kate."

B.J. scanned the list. "Yes, they all have the kind of catchy, provocative names you associate with spy activities,'' he said approvingly. ''Pussy Katz. Kitty Litter. Cozy Knook. Virginity Gonn. Fancy Hooker. Ella Mae Poontang.'' He chuckled.

Dr. Yes leaned forward, curious. ''Does it list their weight?''

Ignoring him, B.J. addressed his brother. ''Are all of these ladies available?''

''To the best of my knowledge, yes.''

B.J. glanced again at the list of names. ''You sure none of these is a guy in drag?''

''Alas, no.''

''We haven't had much luck working with female impersonators lately.''

''I guarantee these are all authentic women.''

The black man tapped the list against his chin. ''I've used Fancy Hooker before. She's very dependable, and mean, too,'' he said. ''Fact is, she used to work as a dominatrix in a swank bordello in New Orleans and got fired because the masochists complained she was too nasty to them.''

''That's Fancy all right,'' said Dr. Maybe. ''Completely heartless.''

''She ought to be perfect for bumping off Triple 'O' Seven.''

''Yes, in some terribly vicious and grisly way.''

''I'll contact her,'' promised B.J., folding up the list.

''Best do it as soon as possible,'' suggested Dr. Yes. ''We want that fellow dead before we conduct our biggest field test yet next week in Los Angeles.''

''I'll get in touch with her and offer my standard deal.''

Dr. Maybe said, ''Fancy's very fussy, B.J. You'll have to offer her a bonus, major medical, and all sorts of perks.''

''Okay, okay. Just so she takes care of Triple 'O' Seven for us.''

Dr. Yes heaved up out of his chair. ''I believe—''

The chair started to quiver, followed by the walls and the floor. Yes tumbled back into his seat.

''Heavens to Betsy,'' exclaimed Dr. Maybe, clutching his handkerchief to his chest. ''What's happening?''

Unruffled, B.J. said, ''It's only Mount Noofu, our extinct volcano.''

''Extinct volcanoes don't shake the very earth,'' Dr. Maybe pointed out.

The tremor dimmed and the room ceased jiggling.

''It only causes a little earthquake now and then. Relax.''

Dr. Yes made another attempt to rise, successful this time. ''I believe I'll take my leave.''

''Where are you going?'' asked B.J.

''Merely out for a little snack.''

Chapter 13

NEW YORK CITY

The theater night watchman looked Triple 'O' Seven up and down. "Ain't that something?" he said, scratching at his sparse white hair.

"My papers are all in order."

"Oh, sure. These say you're a reporter with *Showbiz Illustrated* and authorize you to look around inside the George Jessel Theatre," said the old man. "I was just lookin' at your clothes."

"Is there something wrong with my—"

"Nossir, it's only just that you're so dang dapper," answered the watchman. "I ain't seen a well-dressed reporter since Walter Winchell passed on to glory. And one in a dinner jacket . . . danged if that ain't something."

"There's no reason a writer can't be well dressed."

"Try to tell that to some of these young whippersnappers nowadays." He opened the metal backstage door wider.

"C'mon in, Mr. . . ." He consulted the false ID and letter of introduction. "Mr. Scanlon. Scoop Scanlon. Yessir, that's the sort of name a reporter ought to have. Scoop."

"I didn't catch your name."

"Pop."

"I'll just come in and look around, Pop."

Pop stepped aside and Seven entered the dim-lit backstage area.

"Darn shame you couldn't have poked around before they ripped everything up to build that half-wit church on the stage. Spoils the looks of the whole dang—"

"Actually, Pop, the replica of Notre Dame is one of the things I've come to see."

"Suppose so. Guess that atrocity is news." He gestured in the direction of the dimly illuminated stage. "Want I should flip on more lights?"

"No, this'll be fine."

"I'll let you wander around on your own, Scoop." The watchman started shuffling off toward his small office. "I'll listen to my radio and try not to think about how all these newfangled set designers have butchered the theater up."

Seven headed first for the prop room. It was a large, shadowy place, with the carts, crutches, and other props for the Hunchback musical taking up most of the space.

Using a pocket flash, he explored the room.

Near one wall he spotted a coil of rope. It was identical to that which had been used to tie up the professor as well as the shapely Kate Smithsonian.

As Seven straightened up from examining it, his foot bumped against something metallic.

Stooping, he picked up an underarm spray deodorant

can. It was labeled—*Pitstop! The Tough Deodorant for Men & Women*!

"Pitstop? I thought I was aware of just about every grooming product on the market. Never heard of this one, though. Wonder what it smells like." He depressed the nozzle.

Nothing came out but tired air.

"Empty, eh?" On impulse he dropped the can into a trouser pocket, even though it spoiled the lines.

Easing out of the prop room, he headed for the stage.

There, rising up majestically, stood a very convincing replica of the facade of Notre Dame Cathedral. Gargoyles, bell towers, and all.

"Haven't been in Paris for far too long," he said to himself.

Halting in the middle of the stage, he gazed up at the structure.

As he did he saw a heavy sandbag hurtling straight down at him.

Pivoting, Seven dived to his left, landed on the simulated cobblestones, and rolled.

The sandbag landed with a resounding thud less than a yard from him.

From high above came a faint bonging sound—as though someone had bumped into a huge bell.

Seven rolled further, jumped to his feet, and yanked out his Baretta. He dashed behind the facade of the cathedral, started climbing up the intricacy of metal ladders and catwalks that led upward to the bell tower.

Before he reached his goal someone began firing down on him.

"An Iver Johnson Trailsman pistol from the sound of

it,'' he surmised, dodging the slugs and continuing to ascend.

He fired back.

There was a muffled cry of pain.

The sniping from above ceased.

Seven continued, very cautiously, his climb.

Sprawled on the wooden floor of the bell tower was Kate Smithsonian, her right shoulder bleeding and her gun lying near her hand.

''That looks nasty.'' He knelt beside the blonde, appropriating her pistol.

''You're a jinx, damn it.''

''Yes, I've been told that. Even by some of my own colleagues.''

''Every single damn time I try to kill you, I foul it up.''

He nodded sympathetically. ''I'll do the best I can with your wound, but I'm not carrying a very large first-aid kit with me,'' he explained as he tore away the sleeve of her candy-striped blouse. ''I find a large kit tends to spoil the hang of one's dinner jacket.''

''You can't imagine how many people I've flattened out with dropped sandbags,'' she said while he treated the flesh wound. ''When I trailed you in here, I really thought I had you. But no, just another foul-up. I'll tell you something else, Seven. I usually have great luck with that tied-up naked gambit. I've lured several gents to their doom with that one.''

''Perhaps, Kate, you've been too long at the fair.''

''Meaning?''

''It may just be time to retire. I've read your dossier and I'd bet a woman with your talents could find gainful employment in any number of other—''

"No, nope. Espionage is my calling."

"I'd guess you've lost your knack for killing, Kate."

"I have not. Except where you're concerned."

He examined the bandage he'd applied. "Yes, that takes care of it," he informed her. "But we'll have to have a physician take a gander to make sure—"

"What are you going to do with me?"

"Interrogate you. Then we'll—"

"You're not going to interrogate anyone, ducks." Alfred Hawkshaw, a fire ax gripped in both hands, stepped out of the shadows that filled the spaces between the heavy, dangling bells.

Chapter 14

Before Seven could retrieve the pistol he'd set aside while attending to the wounded Kate, Hawkshaw lunged and kicked at it.

The Baretta flew out of the tower and hit the stage floor far below with an echoing whack.

"On your feet and back away from her," ordered the composer/spy.

Seven complied with the orders, moving up and away from the bandaged blonde and backing toward the nearest big bell. It hung at shoulder level.

"I must say," said Hawkshaw to Kate, "that I'm disappointed in you, dear heart."

"Honestly, Alfie, I don't know what's wrong. I've never had this much trouble assassinating anybody before."

"Maybe it's time to put you out to pasture, ducks."

Very gradually Seven was moving his hand toward

Kate's confiscated gun, which he'd thrust in the waistband of his trousers.

"Alfie, you'd better search him," warned Kate. "He took my gun."

"Took your gun, too, did he? Honestly, Katie, you're getting very slipshod." Hawkshaw leaned the ax against the low wall and whipped out a SIG-Sauer P-226 D.A. automatic pistol. "Raise those hands, Mr. Seven."

"Certainly, old man." Obligingly he raised his hands to shoulder level.

"Good thing I decided to drop in at the Jessel tonight to check out this tower for some revisions I'm contemplating for the *Bellringer's Boogie* number." He inched closer to Seven. "Once I frisk you, Mr. Seven, you're going to experience an unfortunate fall from up here. I simply can't wait until Kate gets lucky enough to—"

"Hey, up there! What the dickens are you up to, Scoop?"

It was Pop, yelling from down on the dark stage.

His shout was sufficient to distract Hawkshaw for a few seconds.

Seven took advantage of that. He jumped, caught hold of the suspended bell, and swung on it.

Raising both feet, he went swinging into the distracted Hawkshaw. He booted the composer in the chest.

Hawkshaw tottered, went stumbling backward.

He tripped over the prone Kate, howled, and fell out of the tower.

"Glory be!" exclaimed Pop as Hawkshaw slammed into the stage.

* * *

Seven shifted the unconscious girl to his other shoulder. "Taxi!" he called out.

A moment later a cab pulled up to the curb. The driver was a pale young man clad in a tuxedo. "Need any help with the lady, sir?"

"I can manage, thank you." Seven got the rear door open and deposited the drugged Kate on the backseat. He eased into the yellow taxi and sat beside her.

"Seems to be some fracas over at the George Jessel," mentioned the dapper driver. "Know what's going on? Lots of cops and fire engines."

"I believe their Notre Dame Cathedral set has collapsed."

"No kidding. What'd cause that?"

"They conjecture that someone was fooling with the bells in the tower and weakened the whole structure."

"The vandalism in this damn city is incredible. Well, where to?"

Seven gave him the address of the new East Side hotel he'd checked into earlier in the evening. "You're quite well dressed for a cabbie," he added.

"The company passed a new dress code recently."

"Quite commendable."

The youth shrugged. "I was more comfortable in my bib overalls," he said, activating the meter and urging the cab into the flow of night traffic. "See, I'm a country and western singer."

"Where from?"

"Newark."

"Ah yes, a hotbed of rustic ballads."

"Listen, Ramblin' Bob Weber was born in Baltimore

and he's had three platinum records this year alone. A person doesn't have to be from the country to— Out of the way, peckerhead! You don't have to be from the country to be a hit singer."

"I quite agree. Chap I know from Liverpool is quite good. Even manages to yodel."

"It's not that difficult to yodel. Want to hear me?"

"No," replied Seven politely.

"Yep, lots of people feel that way about my yodeling."

They drove on in silence for nearly ten minutes.

"This is your hotel," the driver announced, pulling up in front of a narrow but ornate hotel. "Need any help toting the lady inside?"

"I can handle her, thanks." Paying him, Seven climbed from the cab and reached inside for Kate. He arranged her again over a shoulder.

The doorman was a husky Hispanic in a crimson and gold uniform. "Carry the young lady for you, sir?"

"No, thanks."

He opened the glass and gilt door, tipped his visored cap.

Seven strolled over to the marbled desk. "My key, please."

The perfumed clerk was perusing an interior decorating magazine, making pleased chuckling sounds. "This is my dream house," he announced, pointing at a photo with a manicured finger.

"Pink and peach are certainly your colors," commented Seven. "My key?"

"Oh yes, sorry." He abandoned the magazine, reluctantly, to fetch the key. "Shall I summon one of our muscular bellhops to help with your companion?"

"Won't be necessary." Grinning amiably, he pocketed the key and crossed to the elevator.

The operator was a hefty, gray-haired woman of sixty. She yawned twice before asking, "What floor?"

"Thirteen."

The woman shuddered. "Boy, you wouldn't catch me staying on that floor. It's a hoodoo."

"I don't subscribe to that superstition."

"Neither did the dozens of guests who've come to grief on the thirteenth over the years."

The elevator cage rattled and moaned as it climbed upward.

"Here you are, accursed thirteen. Good luck."

"Much obliged." He transferred Kate to his arms and carried her out into the maroon-carpeted corridor.

His room was 1313.

Getting the door open, he crossed the threshold with his burden.

All the lights in the living room blossomed before he could even reach for a switch.

A grim Oriental youth in a black Ninja uniform and hood was standing in the center of the room, brandishing a wicked-looking kris knife. "Please come all the way in, Mr. Seven," he invited, "so that I may send you off to visit your ancestors."

Chapter 15

WASHINGTON, D.C.

The senior presidential adviser had misplaced the president again. He was searching the night corridors of the White House, quietly calling out, "Mr. President? Mr. President?"

He found him in the kitchen, sitting in a wooden chair. There was a thoughtful look on the lined old face of the chief executive as he sat toying with the belt of his flannel bathrobe. "What's the name of that feller with the mustache?"

The heavyset adviser hesitated in the doorway. "Where'd you get to, sir? I was all ready to tuck you in and then, while I was filling your hot-water bottle, you wandered off."

"Wasn't a big mustache." The president of the United States held a quivering finger over his upper lip. "Little bitty mustache."

"You mean General Ganso y Pato? You met with him in the Rose Garden this afternoon and promised him three million dollars to help him wipe out the Antigasozas in his crucial Central American country, which is one of the last bastions of democ—"

"No, no, this feller wore a derby and walked like a pansy."

"I don't recall anyone of that description visiting the White House recently, Mr. Sandcastle."

President Ricardo Sandcastle shook his head, his silvery locks flickering. "No, no, I mean a feller I used to know in Hollywood," he said, eyeing his adviser and frowning. "Come to think of it—what's your name?"

"I'd rather not say." Blushing, the adviser looked down at his highly polished shoes. "It's an embarrassing name and—"

"This is your commander in chief asking you."

"Well, it's Watergate, sir. Wally Watergate. If it wasn't that my dear old father was so proud of the family name, I'd change it to—"

"This feller I'm trying to recollect, Wally, was in the flickers same time as I was. Derby, mustache, cane."

"Warner Baxter?"

President Sandcastle thought for a moment. "Nope."

"Ronald Colman?"

"Nope. This was a much funnier feller than Ronald Colman."

"Clark Gable?"

"Did he have a mustache? Anyway, he was after my time. You got to keep in mind, Wally, that I was one of the great *silent* movie idols." The old man sighed. "When

I made *The Tent of the Sheik* in 1927, women all over the nation—what did they call young women back then?''

''Bobby-soxers?''

''No, no, this was in the 1920s.''

''Flappers?''

''Flappers, that's right. Millions of flappers adored me. When I rode in on that white stallion and bared my chest to the captive English girl, that was a great moment in cinema—up to that time.''

Watergate, very politely, cleared his throat. ''Any reason why you're in the kitchen, sir, at this hour?''

''Trying to remember the name of that feller with the derby.''

''Couldn't you do that in bed? I want to brief you, before you fall asleep, on the matter of a possible new threat to civilization as we know—''

''Charlie. Charlie something.''

''Chaplin?''

President Sandcastle pondered. ''Might've been,'' he decided finally. ''Charlie Chaplin. Whatever happened to him?''

''Passed away, sir. Now, about that CIA report on a potential plague of uncontrollable horniness that may sweep—''

''They're all dying off. Jack Gilbert, Rudy Valentino. It's sad.''

''You must keep in mind, Mr. President, that you've been fortunate enough to live far beyond the allotted span.''

''What did I tell you about bringing up my age . . . Willie, is it?''

"Close, sir. It's Wally."

"Wally." The president nodded. "If I go for a third term, I don't want to hear people around here mentioning the fact that I'm . . . How old am I exactly?"

"Ninety-six."

"Really? Isn't that something."

Edging closer to the chief executive, Watergate said, "Time to get to bed. It's nearly nine."

"I'm going to make all the record books, Willie. First silent movie star ever to be president of the United States. First man over the age of ninety to be elected to the office. Um . . . maybe I'd rather not they remind people of that." He rested his knobby hands on his bony knees. "We ought to run *The Return of the Sheik* some night. That's the one where I kidnap Mary Astor and ride with her across the burning sands to my oasis."

"There are no prints of that film in existence, sir. They all disintegrated a long time ago."

" 'I'll tame you 'ere the sun sets on these burning sands, my fair golden-haired flower!' That's what I tell her as I carry her into the tent. A great moment in the history of the cinema."

"So I've heard." Carefully, Watergate took hold of the president's left elbow. "Would you like me to fix you a cup of cocoa?"

"Ovaltine."

The adviser let go of him and moved toward one of the stoves. "You rest right here, and I'll fix you a mug."

"You've got to stop harping on the fact I need rest, Willis. For a man my age, I happen to be exceptionally spry—How old did you say I was?"

"Ninety-six."

The president gave a pleased chuckle. "That's amazing," he said admiringly. "Ninety-six and still fighting the enemies of democracy and decency, especially those greaseballs down in Latin America."

Watergate coughed. "Sir, you agreed not to refer to Latin Americans, friend or foe, as greaseballs or greasers."

"So I did. Sorry, Walter," he said. "We always called them that in my westerns. *Deputy Sheriff of Devil's Doorknob, The Lone Rider of—*"

"The CIA is going to be taking action on this latest threat to Western civilization, sir. In fact," said Watergate as he lifted a container of Ovaltine off a shelf, "one of our men is set to interface with a British agent in Manhattan this very evening."

". . .*Tombstone Territory*," concluded President Sandcastle. "That was my best cowboy flicker. When I tipped my sombrero and went riding away from the schoolmarm's fresh-dug grave—wellsir, it was another great moment in the history of cinema."

"Do you want a marshmallow in your Ovaltine?"

"Let me think about that for a moment," requested the president.

Chapter 16

NEW YORK CITY

Triple 'O' Seven raised his voice. "Is that better, Y?"

"A bit, yes. Where the devil are you telephoning from? Sounds like they're smashing glass in the background."

"Yes, some chaps seem to be breaking into a liquor store across the way."

"You mean to say you're calling me from a pay phone on the streets of Manhattan, Seven?"

"Yes, and I've had a rough time finding one that works."

"Aren't you going to be late for your rendezvous with that CIA bloke?"

"A bit, yes. But I thought I'd best take time to explain the bill you'll be getting for the float."

"What float?"

"It apparently—although I only viewed it after the Ninja assassin had landed squarely on the thing—depicted St.

Norbert the Chaste driving the weasels out of Lithuania. All made of fresh flowers and chicken wire."

"We're being sent a bill for this monstrosity?"

"A monstrosity perhaps, Y, yet an important part of tomorrow's St. Norbert's Day parade," explained Seven. "As fate would have it, the float was passing beneath the window of my hotel room just as the Ninja assassin fell."

"Then let the damn Ninja assassins foot the bill for—"

"He fell, sir, as a direct result of a few Oriental fighting tricks I picked up in Chinatown while visiting San Francisco the summer before—"

"Can't you simply disable these fellows? Must you continually defenestrate them? I suppose we'll have to kick in for a broken window as well?"

Seven nodded at the phone. "A window, sir, the drapes, and an accordian."

"An accordian, old man?"

"A previous tenant left it behind in the room and when the Ninja assassin took his fall, he somehow managed to take the accordian with him. A very handsome one with *Property of Orlando Busino* emblazoned on its front in pearl studs and—"

"Any other charges of which I ought to be informed?"

"Only the cost of the room at the Ethel M. Dell Hotel for Women."

"Why are we renting a room at—"

"I needed someplace to store Kate Smithsonian. She's unconscious and, for good measure, bound and gagged. I suggest you rush a man over there to . . . No, wait. On second thought, send a female agent. They raised quite a row when I carried her up to the room. Seems they have some rule about men not being allowed above the—"

"Any notion, Seven, why this Ninja chap was out to kill you?"

"We actually didn't get much chance to talk. I assume, however, it all ties in with this Underfoot affair."

"Very well, and now I suggest you get on your way to your meeting with the CIA."

"I shall, sir," promised Seven. "Allow me just to mention that I won't even go into the damages at the George Jessel Theatre, since I don't believe there's any way we can be held responsible for the Cathedral of Notre Dame collapsing like that."

"Tell me all about it at some future date," said Y as he hung up.

Triple 'O' Seven strolled along the quiet, tree-lined East Side street until he came to the address he was seeking. He climbed the steps to the white door of the narrow three-story town house. After glancing around, he rang the bell.

High overhead a jetliner went winging through the night.

Seven tried the bell once again.

"Oh, darn, hold on," said someone inside.

It was a woman's voice.

He heard her swearing to herself—"Hot damn, son of a biscuit, flapping A John Tweedy"—and grunting.

"Is something wrong, miss?"

"Just keep your drawers on, okay?"

A bit more grunting and cursing—"Diddlywacker, mammyjammer, hackensacker"—and then the chain rattled out of its slot and the door opened about seven inches.

A very pretty young woman looked out at him. There was a feverish cast to her tanned face and her red hair was tangled. "This is really dippy," she said, "but could you, please, shove at the door real hard?"

"I could, yes."

"Well, then do it for cripesakes."

Obligingly the mustached agent put a broad shoulder to the wood and pushed. "Seems to be giving a bit."

"Yeah, yep, that's fine. Keep it up." When the reluctant door was two feet open the feverish redhead invited, "Come on in."

"I have an appointment with Bubber Kapusky and . . . Oops." He noticed that what was blocking the door was a chunky, gray-haired man who was sprawled on the marble floor of the foyer.

"That's just Bascom," explained the pretty young woman, adjusting a strap of her green silk evening dress. "The butler or something like that."

Seven crouched down beside the unconscious man. "What's wrong with him?"

"Not a blessed thing actually. Except I didn't think the knockout drug would work so fast on him. Otherwise I wouldn't have used it so close to the door."

"You've drugged this poor chap?"

She nodded, causing the other strap to slip. "See, I'm not used to this sort of work," she confided. "Nope, but Daddy insisted I handle it. He's grooming me, even though I'm a female, to take over the whole darn business eventually."

"What sort of business would that be?" He straightened up and moved away from the fallen butler.

"Hey, don't you recognize me?"

He scanned her. "I fear not."

"Don't you, hey, read *People, Time, Newsweek, Vanity*

Fair, Life, New York . . . excuse me.'' She reached around him to push the door shut. ''. . . the New York *Post, Interview*, the *Village*—''

''None of them regularly, no. I don't suppose you've been written up in *Foreign Affairs*?''

''Not yet.'' She shrugged and both straps slid down her smooth tan shoulders. ''Okay, well, since you don't recognize me, I'll tell you. I'm Bitchy Sue Bedrock.''

''Pleased to meet you, Miss Bedrock. Is Bubber Kapusky at home?''

''Son of a biscuit. You still don't realize who I am,'' she said, nonplussed. ''Darn, seducing you's going to be even trickier than I figured. I'm Bitchy Sue Bedrock, only daughter of T. Texas Bedrock. Daddy happens to be the fourth—or maybe it's the fifth, since some of the other contenders are challenging his claim—richest man in America. He owns International Toiletries.''

''Yes, I recognize the name,'' Seven replied politely. ''I'm already late for my meeting with Bubber Kapusky, so if you'd—''

''Leaping lizards, I am really not handling this at all well.'' Bitchy Sue took a few steps backward. ''See, I . . . You are Triple 'O' Seven, aren't you?''

''I am, yes.''

''Good. That's a dippy name, by the way.''

''We can't all be named Bitchy Sue Bedrock.''

''I think my name's catchy. So do dozens of satisfied suitors.''

''Where's Kapusky?''

''Kapusky's in an unconscious state off in the living room.'' She pointed in that direction. ''Would you like to take a swim?''

"No."

"I mentioned that because there's a terrific indoor swimming pool in the basement. And a harp on the second floor."

Seven asked, "How does Bubber Kapusky come to be out cold, Miss Bedrock?"

"I drugged him, too." She reached one slender tan hand into the cleavage of her dress and drew out a hypodermic needle. "Darn thing feels awful cold on my yonkers."

"Am I to assume, since you seem to have rendered a CIA agent unconscious, that you are affiliated with the KGB?"

"Of course not, don't be dippy. What Daddy and I represent is the spirit of free enterprise," she explained. "Once Daddy gets hold of this Underfoot formula, he'll turn it into a multimillion dollar product. Minute he heard of it, he knew International Toiletries had to have it. It's absolutely dippy to use the stuff for political purposes. If Daddy'd known about the stuff before Underfoot made his deal with these political people, he'd have topped any offer."

"Did you expect to find the Underfoot formula here?"

"Heck, no. I expected to find you here, Triple." Her nose wrinkled. "Is that what your cronies call you?"

"Some."

"Dippy." She paused, took a deep breath. Both straps of her gown slipped again. "Well, okay, let's get down to the seduction. We can use the master bedroom, or the water bed in the guest room or—if you go in for that sort of thing—a bearskin rug in the den. Not much of a bear, if you ask me, with moth holes and a serious overbite, but—"

"Why are you contemplating seducing me, Miss Bedrock?"

"Could you call me Bitchy Sue? Since we'll soon be between the old sheets, it—"

"You haven't answered my question, Bitchy Sue."

"Well, everybody knows you're susceptible to lovely women, of which I am a prime example." She held her arms wide. The straps fell again and the dress slipped down to reveal two small but exceptionally appealing breasts. "Ignore that, the seduction hasn't officially begun." She tugged the top of the gown back into place.

Grinning, Seven told her, "You people are forever confusing me with my father. I am certainly interested in attractive young ladies, and I agree that you're an excellent example of the genre, but I cannot be seduced or romanced off the track. The siren song of even the most beautiful spy on the face of the earth wouldn't lure me from my duty as—"

"I'm not a spy, darn it," she said, angry. "Well, maybe a sort of industrial spy, but not the cloak-and-dagger kind. Daddy and I simply want to persuade you to turn the Underfoot formula over to us once you locate it, Triple."

"What makes you think I'll find it?"

"Oh, we ran the names of all the darn agents involved in this hunt through our computer—and you came in first," she said. "Well, no. Actually you came in second, but the number one guy is with the Vatican and I'm not about to vamp a clerical person."

"I appreciate your confidence," he said. "But I can't deal with you or with International Toiletries. My path as an agent of Her Majesty has not always been smooth, yet

I've never been distracted by a pretty face or a mess of porridge."

"I thought that was pottage."

"Neither would tempt me from my sworn duty."

"Darn, I'm truly sorry to hear that," she said, giving a sad shake of the head. "Because I'm already tired of drugging people around this place. Besides Bascom and Bubber, there was the cook, the upstairs maid, the downstairs maid, some gink who came to tune the harp, and a very mean-minded bulldog."

His grin broadened. "You can't, surely, think you're going to be able to attack me with that hypo?"

"No, I can't. For you, Triple, I'm relying on that gas that is, even as we speak, swirling out of that vent just above your handsome head." She smiled, tapping the side of her pretty nose. "I have a miniature gas mask stuffed up here."

"Just a min . . ." He had the impression someone had suddenly dropped a funeral wreath around his neck. His eyes snapped shut, his knees buckled, he fell atop the butler.

Chapter 17

TANGIER, MOROCCO

The overhead fan in the shadowy bedchamber of the suite at the fashionable Hotel Hashara made a mournful chuffing sound. The extremely lovely raven-haired woman who lay naked on the luxurious canopied bed paused in her reading to give the fan an annoyed glance.

Returning to the sheaf of letters in her hands, she commenced reading. " 'All you must do, esteemed Miss Hooker, is . . .' Where's that frigging code book for the White Supremacy Secret Army of Africa? It's red, right? Not this one, not this one . . . this isn't red, it's maroon. Okay, here it is. 'All you must do, esteemed Miss Hooker, is assassinate the prime minister of North Nafaka, for which we'll gladly pay you the princely sum of . . .' " She flipped through the pages of the small, red-covered codebook. " 'The princely sum of forty thousand dollars.' Nertz. What prince would work for a measly sum like that?'' Fancy Hooker crumpled the letter, tossed it and the red-covered codebook over the side of her bed, where it joined a scatter of other missives and codebooks.

She scratched briefly at her handsome left breast, glared once more at the noisy fan, and then picked up another job offer. ''These dimbulbs didn't even bother to write in code. 'Will pay you twenty-five thousand dollars for ruining the reputation of the Archbishop of Achterwaarts.' '' Tapping her chin with the letter, she grew thoughtful. ''I could do that in a couple days tops. Naw, it's worth at least forty thousand dollars.'' The letter was crumpled and jettisoned.

A knock sounded on the door.

Fancy ignored it.

'' 'Esteemed Ms. Hooker: We would appreciate an estimate as to how much you would charge to whip and humiliate us.' Where've these dumbbunnies been? I quit the dominatrix racket nearly three years ago.''

The knocking came again.

''What already?'' she yelled.

''It's a singing telegram, Miss Hooker.''

''Get lost, kiddo.''

More knocking.

Muttering, Fancy got out from under the scatter of remaining inquiries, offers, and invitations and left her bed. Unclothed, she padded to the door. ''This better be important,'' she said, yanking it open.

A slim, blond young woman with a telegram clutched in her hand stood on the threshold. ''This is a birthday greeting, Miss Hooker. Perhaps you'd like to slip into something appropriate for the occas—''

"It isn't my birthday, bimbo. Take a hike."

Emily Watts-Batsfree thrust her booted foot into the opening and prevented the door from being slammed shut. "I really think you ought to hear this."

"Scram."

"Sighing, Emily bent and whipped a small, odd-shaped pistol out of her thigh holster.

Katang!

She shot a dart into Fancy's bare midsection.

"Don't tell me I'm being assassinated? That'd be ironic as . . ." Her eyes blanked, her mouth snapped shut. She knelt and then slowly fell over sideways.

Emily eased into the room.

After holstering the gun that had delivered a shot of knockout drug to the notorious free-lance secret agent, she shut the door of the hotel suite. She got hold of the unconscious Fancy by the armpits and dragged her farther into the room.

"That'll do," she said, spotting a large steamer trunk against the wall.

In less than five minutes she had Fancy stowed away inside the trunk.

"I really am getting into a rut," she observed as she sat down in front of the makeup mirror. "Only a few days ago I popped poor Triple 'O' Seven into a similar trunk."

She took a small disguise kit from the bosom of her fashionable frock and set to work. It took her only a few moments to convert herself into a reasonable facsimile of Fancy Hooker.

Another minute passed and then there came a knock upon the door.

"Yes?"

"It is I, Miss Hooker," said an oily voice. "Dr. Ludwig Pesticide."

"Yes, Doctor. I've been expecting you," said Emily, rising.

Kaboom!

Dr. Pesticide pursed his ruby-red lips, gave a disapproving nod of his head. His multiple jowls quivered, the tassle on his crimson fez swished. "These terrorists, gad, they make dining at an outdoor café extremely annoying at times."

Emily, now a replica of Fancy Hooker, watched the remains of the exploded diplomatic limousine come raining down out of the hot afternoon sky and clunk and clatter on the sun-bright sidewalk across the narrow Tangier street from the Café Ahmar. "Quit getting distracted, fatty," she advised, "and get down to business."

He was an enormous man in a wilted white suit and all but one of his fat fingers was decorated with a bejeweled ring. "I admire your frankness, my dear, indeed I do," he told her with a wheezy laugh. "I can see why Jobb is anxious to employ you."

"So get to the—"

"Allah! What is this I find in my soup?" suddenly shouted a burnoosed businessman at a nearby outdoor table.

A gaunt waiter in a tan caftan came over to him. "Ah, it appears to be a spark plug, sir."

"Well, remove it at once, pig!"

"Have a care, sir, as to whom you address as pig."

"Pig!"

"Aaaiiii!" The waiter jerked a formidable kirs from beneath his robe and attacked the complaining customer.

"Honestly," said Dr. Pesticide, "the people in this godforsaken city are the most hot-tempered lot I've—"

"What's B.J. offering me?"

"The chance to perform a service for the cause of—"

"Nix, fatso. I mean what's the damn salary?"

"You must realize, Miss Hooker, that these are troubled times. The overhead in the espionage trade is always on the rise and therefore—"

"How much?"

"Forty thousand dollars."

"Nertz. I can get almost that much for ruining a bishop."

"Fifty thousand dollars."

Emily tapped her fingernail on the lip of her cocktail glass. "Let me see if I have this assignment straight," she said slowly. "I'm to track down this British agent called Triple 'O' Seven and terminate him. Is that pretty much it?"

"Exactly. You can see how simple it is."

"How come so many of Jobb's other people have failed, if it's such a cinch?"

"Very well, sixty thousand dollars."

"A hundred thousand dollars."

"Quite quite impossible. Seventy-five thousand."

"Ninety thousand at least."

"Eighty thousand," countered the fat man. "Not a penny more."

Emily scowled thoughtfully for almost a full minute. "Okay, it's a deal. But I still think B.J.'s a cheap son of a bitch."

Dr. Pesticide gestured at the remains of the limo. ‘‘There are many, many in this world who'll kill for far less.’’

‘‘So hire yourself a couple of loonies to do in Seven.’’

‘‘We prefer you, dear child.’’

‘‘Okay, I want forty thousand dollars deposited in my account in Switzerland,’’ she told him. ‘‘Do that today.’’

‘‘It shall be done.’’

‘‘Now, give me some more details on this whole affair.’’

‘‘Very well,’’ said the fat man.

Chapter 18

LONG ISLAND SOUND

Triple 'O' Seven awoke in darkness.

A thick, tight darkness that smelled somewhat of moldering potatoes.

"In a sack," he realized. "Yes, that's it all right. I'm inside a burlap sack, tied hand and foot with what feels like plastic clothesline."

He became aware, as his head cleared, that he and his potato sack were on a carpeted floor and that the floor was, gently, rocking from side to side.

"At sea," Seven concluded. "I've been shanghaied."

No use lamenting or speculating further. The thing to do was get free.

Seven twisted as best he could under the circumstances and attempted to reach the heel of his left shoe with the fingers of his right hand. There was a small, extremely sharp little blade concealed in the hollow of the heel.

Gasping, grunting, he twisted and stretched. Finally, after several uncomfortable minutes, he got hold of the shoe and gave the heel a twist.

Nothing happened. The heel wouldn't budge.

"Jammed, blast it."

Well, there were, fortunately, alternatives.

For instance, stitched in the lining of the breast pocket of his dinner jacket was another tiny, razor-sharp blade. Seven was of the opinion that it spoiled the hang of the jacket, but the blade had come in handy in previous emergencies.

"Going to be damned difficult, however, to get my tied hands around from behind my back and anywhere near my breast pocket."

The acid fountain pen might be able to eat through the clothesline.

"But that's in my breast pocket, too."

While he was reviewing his options, he gave the shoe heel another jerk. The heel didn't budge, but the whole shoe came off in his fist.

Then Seven remembered that there was a small Ninja star concealed in a secret pocket in the toe of his sock.

The problem was to get the sock off his foot.

He managed to shift his position enough so that he could catch hold of the elastic of the sock. Slowly, painfully, he peeled the stocking from his foot.

He reeled in the sock, felt at the toe end.

"That's odd."

There was no Ninja star. There wasn't even a secret pocket.

Seven paused, thinking hard.

"Knife in the heel of the left shoe. Star in the toes of . . . Ah, but of course. Star in the *right* sock."

He and his sack thumped on the ship's cabin floor as Seven rolled around to get in a position where he could take off his right shoe.

One increasing problem was the fact that he'd been tied up very tightly, affecting his circulation. His fingers were growing numb with the passing of time.

"Well," he told himself, "no use complaining."

He was able to work the second shoe off in what he estimated was about five minutes.

The sock he removed in roughly three.

Seven had just gotten the sharp-edged star in his hand when something yanked him and his sack up off the swaying floor and carried them away.

"You could've been a bit more careful, Miss Bedrock," said Seven as he stepped free of the sack and shed the last of the ropes.

"Quit bitching. I only made a dinky tear in your dinner jacket while I was cutting you loose."

He took a few tentative steps across the deck of the cruising yacht. His legs were somewhat numb and his movements wobbly. "Had you not trussed me up like a Boxing Day present in the first place I'd—"

"Nertz to you."

"This sure sounds like a budding romance to me." T. Texas Bedrock was sitting in a canvas chair near the bow rail of his yacht. Even in the thin light of dawn he had a ruddy look. He was about sixty, deeply tanned and wearing a blazer, white duck trousers, and a yachting cap. "Most of my wives and I squabbled just like you two during the courting stages. It's a sure sign of affection and suppressed lust."

"Oh, baloney," commented his daughter, settling into a canvas chair and keeping her Raven MP-25 automatic pistol aimed at Seven.

He did a few simple limbering-up exercises to stimulate his circulation, noticing that they seemed to be traveling along about two miles off the Long Island coast. "I am, Mr. Bedrock, an employee of the British government," he said evenly. "You and your scatterbrained daughter have kidnapped me, shanghaied me, and—"

"Nossir, all we did was invite you to a little business conference," corrected the president of International Toiletries. "True, since little Bitchy Sue's got a crush on you, she got a bit overzealous in persuading you to attend."

"Is that how she behaves when she's overzealous—ties fellows up and encloses them in gunny sacks?"

"You're lucky I didn't stick you in a plastic garbage bag with leftover pizza and a dead cat."

"Sit down, Mr. Seven," invited Bedrock, gesturing at the third canvas chair on the early morning deck.

"I prefer to stand, thank you."

"Care for a spot of breakfast?"

"No."

"Everybody ought to have some bran in the morning."

"Even so."

Bedrock nodded at his daughter. "You can lower the gun, Bitchy Sue honey."

"I may want to shoot him."

"Now now, we don't shoot people at business conferences."

Making a snarling noise, she rested the automatic on her knee. She was dressed in an outfit similar to her father's.

"My proposition is simple, Seven." He reached under his chair, came up with the *Pitstop*! can. "I want the formula for this stuff."

Seven slapped at his coat pocket. "You took that from me while I was unconscious."

"That we did. Along with a fountain pen full of acid and a teeny-weeny knife." Bedrock pointed at the deodorant can. "Up until I found this on you, we weren't certain how they were testing the stuff."

Seven flexed his fingers, finding that they were growing less numb. "Surely you must realize, Mr. Bedrock, that in the wrong hands the Underfoot formula might well spell disaster for the whole world. Societies wherein the population concentrates too much on sensual activities do not thrive."

"We don't consider ourselves," put in Bitchy Sue, "as the wrong hands, dummy."

"The stuff the KGB is using on unsuspecting victims is much too strong, Seven," said her father. "The product I have in mind will be watered down and much milder."

"Can't you," inquired Seven, "determine the formula by analyzing the traces in that can?"

Bedrock shook his head. "Had one of my lab boys try that very thing while you were snoozing," he said. "Turns out there are a couple of secret ingredients—so we must find either Underfoot himself or his formula."

Seven moved casually over to the railing and leaned an elbow on it. He was still shoeless and sockless and the deck was chill beneath his bare feet. "It is my opinion, sir, that the world is better off without the Underfoot formula,'' he told the tycoon. ''When I find Underfoot, it shall be my duty to destroy the formula and persuade him not to try again.''

''Ethics,'' commented Bitchy Sue. ''Hooey.''

''Ethics are swell,'' said her father, ''but so's common sense, Seven. I'm willing to pay you a hundred thousand dollars for the formula. All you'll have to do, my boy, is slip me a photocopy of the damn thing. You can burn the original, brainwash Underfoot—whatever'll make you feel good.''

''Out of the question.''

''Look at it this way,'' he said. ''Sooner or later my lab people will crack the secret anyway. So the most you can hope for is a delay.''

''There is no possibility of my doing business with you, sir.''

''How dippy,'' remarked Bitchy Sue as she crossed her legs.

''Two hundred thousand dollars.'' Bedrock leaned forward, watching Seven.

Seven appeared to grow thoughtful. ''I haven't had a chance to look at the exchange rate this morning, but that sounds like it would be a tidy sum in pounds. Enough, perhaps, to buy a cozy cottage in Barsetshire where I might get to work on my thesis on the novels of William LeQueux. Yes, that's tempting . . .'' He took hold of the railing with his right hand, gazing off at Long Island.

''I'll make the price for the formula two hundred fifty thousand dollars,'' said Bedrock. ''You can get a bigger cottage.''

"And perhaps a few sheep," said Seven.

All at once he vaulted over the rail and down toward the gray waters of the Sound.

He hit the chill water with an enormous splash, sank down several yards.

He stayed underwater and began doing a powerful breast stroke.

He surfaced a few minutes later, some distance from the International Toiletries yacht.

On the deck the anxious Bedrock was shouting, "I'll raise it to three hundred thousand!"

Seven submerged again and kept on toward the distant shore of early morning Long Island.

Chapter 19

NEW YORK CITY

Y was holding a toasted bagel in his mittened hand. "Gad, what happened to you, Seven?" he inquired as the agent entered the ice box. "You look as though you spent the night in a burlap sack and then went swimming while fully clothed."

"Well, I spent the night in a burlap sack," replied Seven, seating himself on the pickle barrel. "Then I went swimming while fully clothed."

"Ah, then that explains why I never received your report on your meeting with the CIA chap."

"Precisely. Fact is, I never had the meeting." He reached, gingerly, into a bedraggled pocket of his wrinkled, sodden dinner jacket. "Before I report on what befell me, sir, I'll turn these invoices over to you."

Y accepted the handful of bills, reluctantly. "How did

you manage to run up all these expenses while inside a bag?"

"These costs came up after I emerged."

Frowning, Y read the topmost sheet. "Six hundred dollars for rental of the *Bird of Dawning*? What in blazes is the—"

"A ferryboat, sir. I chanced to come ashore in the pleasant beach town of Port Jefferson, Long Island. The quickest, surest way to get to Manhattan was by ferry. Thus I rented one of the sturdy boats that plies the Sound."

"You could've taken a train."

"The Long Island Railroad is too undependable."

"Twelve hundred dollars for repairs to the *Mary Jane Bisby*?"

"A garbage scow."

"And?"

"We rammed her."

"Seems to me that's an expense this . . . this *Bird of Dawning* ought to foot."

"I neglected to mention that I was at the helm of the ferryboat. I've had quite a bit of experience handling—"

"Eight hundred forty dollars for Rufus Perryman's leg?"

"Wooden leg."

"Who might Rufus Perryman be?"

"I told him to put his rank on the bill, but he neglected to do that. He happens to be the captain of the *Mary Jane Bisby*."

"What, exactly, did you do to the man's leg?"

"Nary a thing, sir. Captain Perryman detached it and threw it at me after I rammed his scow and caused those barrels of toxic waste to fall overboard and sink in the sea."

"The leg, I take it, also sank?"

"Yes, though I would've expected a wooden leg to float," said Seven, rubbing his chilled hands together. "Captain Perryman was already in a black mood because he's been at sea in that scow for two months. There's some debate going on as to whether he can dump the sort of waste he's—"

"Four hundred eight dollars for clams?"

"That was after we went aground."

"You spent four hundred eight dollars for breakfast?"

"No, I inadvertently bumped into the outdoor dining dock attached to Moby Nick's Seaside Clam Shack. The clams for today had just been delivered and were sitting on the dock."

"Into the sea?"

"The majority of them, yes."

Letting the bills fall to the desktop, Y said, "I do hope that you're making some progress on this Underfoot affair."

"I am," Seven assured him. "Finish your bagel and I'll fill you in on all I've learned."

Seven, as he left the delicatessen, glanced at his watch. He had over two hours before his new appointment with Bubber Kapusky of the CIA. Since the afternoon was clear and pleasant, he decided he had time to walk across Central Park to the latest hotel he was residing at, change into more presentable attire, and get to his meeting.

Two plump joggers in maroon warm-up suits ran by him

as he entered the park. He went striding along a wide paved path that cut through the grassy fields and stands of trees. A fat lady on roller skates passed him, and from a horse-drawn carriage a tourist couple snapped photos.

Seven walked at a brisk pace, whistling an old English country tune.

"If the fate of Western civilization wasn't hanging in the balance," he said to himself, "one might actually relax and enjoy such a day as this."

A string of six enthusiastic bicyclers went rolling by, followed by a barking mongrel.

Seven's left shoulder hunched twice. He frowned. For nearly the past two minutes he'd had the feeling he was being followed.

Casually he slowed, stopped, and knelt. While pretending to tie his shoe, he glanced back. A platinum blond was pushing a baby carriage, a black man in an overcoat was talking to a squirrel. There was no one else close behind him.

Straightening, he resumed his walk.

After a moment he left the path and cut up across the grass toward a scatter of oak trees.

A bearded young man was sprawled on the grass, face-up, reciting a prayer in Latin.

Seven worked his way through the trees and then dodged behind one. From a pocket of his rumpled jacket he took a long-handled dental mirror. He stuck it out around the edge of the sturdy oak, tilted in such a way that he could get a look at the ground he'd covered.

He caught a brief glimpse of a dark-haired young woman in a plaid miniskirt and cable-stitch sweater ducking behind a tree.

"Something vaguely familiar about that young lady," he reflected, dropping to his knees.

He eased around his tree, chancing a direct look down at the oak that concealed the dark-haired woman who was apparently tailing him.

No one else was in sight, and she was still behind the other tree.

Shooting to his feet, he ran downhill. He drew the Baretta he'd borrowed from Y to replace the one the Bedrocks had relieved him of aboard their yacht.

"If you'll just keep both hands plainly in view, miss," he ordered as she stepped around the tree and pointed his gun at the girl.

"Honestly, Trip, you're going to throw a spanner in the works."

His left eye narrowed. "Emily?"

"Quick, put your weapon away, pretend you didn't spot me," the disguised Emily urged him. "Then get back to strolling. I'll pretend I'm still tracking you and maybe we—"

"Dark hair isn't at all becoming to you."

"This is a disguise," she explained, anxiously looking back over her shoulder. "When P got word that Fancy Hooker was going to be hired by B. Jobb to kill you, I scooted over to Morocco and drugged her. After stashing her in a trunk, I took her place. Wearing this wig and suitable clothes, I met B.J.'s emissary, a loathsome man named Dr. Ludwig Pesticide, and was given the assignment in her stead. In talking with the man I was able to learn a good deal about their plans to use the Underfoot formula to undermine Western civilization as we know it. I arrived in New York City only this morning, picked up your trail, and have been trailing you ever since. Apparently, however, Jobb doesn't trust me completely and I'm nearly certain he has assigned two thick-necked fellows in crimson running suits to follow me to make sure I follow you and bring off your assassination. Now, Trip, that's really all I have time to tell you right now. Start moving, before those chaps realize what's up and—''

Kachow!

Kachowie!

Two slugs whistled across the afternoon and thunked into the tree trunk a few inches from their respective heads.

''It's my guess they're suspicious already.'' Seven grabbed her hand and they started running.

Halfway down the green hill Seven scooped up Emily and commenced carrying her. ''We can make better time this way,'' he explained, kicking up his running pace.

''There you go again, Trip,'' she said, panting slightly. ''Treating women as though they're inferior and not capable of holding their own.''

From behind them came three more pistol shots.

''Not at all,'' he assured her. ''I'm certain that under different circumstances you might be perfectly capable of picking me up and carrying me.''

Two more shots, neither of which hit them.

''Ah, this ought to come in handy.''

A horse-drawn carriage was parked just below them, its driver nowhere in sight.

He dumped Emily into it, untethered the horse, and hopped up into the driver's seat. ''I'll drive,'' he said. ''Giddyup there, Dobbin.''

The horse whinnied, lurched, and started off at a gallop.

''See what you keep doing, Trip?'' She was hunkered

down below her seat. "Assuming that you're more capable of piloting this thing."

"I'll pop on this top hat the driver left behind. Look more like the real thing that . . . Oops!"

A shot from the gun of one of their cursing pursuers hit the rusty topper, carried it right off Seven's head.

He urged the gray mare to increase its speed and they began to move more rapidly across Central Park, away from the assassins.

Chapter 20

Emily, no longer wearing the black wig, was sitting on the edge of the huge heart-shaped water bed. "What's that you asked, Y?" she was saying into the pink bedside telephone.

"I asked what that awful din was at your end."

"That's Triple," she explained, frowning in the direction of the crimson bathroom door, which was partially open. "Singing in the shower."

"Are you in some sort of compromising position, child?"

"Not at all."

"Whatever is that he's singing?"

"A medley, as he explained it to me, of Burl Ives favorites."

"I see." Y cleared his throat. "Continue with your report."

"I'm abandoning the Fancy Hooker persona," she said, "since the opposition seems to have penetrated my cover."

"The original Fancy Hooker wasn't in that trunk when our chaps went to pick it up in Tangier. I was expecting something like this."

"Trip will be meeting the CIA man in about twenty minutes," she went on. "Meanwhile, he's suggested I pass on the latest expenditures to you so that—"

"More expenses? The chap only left me a bit over an hour ago. How on earth did he—"

"He has a knack, sir," Emily said, opening the tiny notebook that rested on one pretty knee. "Just keep in mind that many great men have tragic flaws."

"Tragic I could live with, but expensive is another thing altogether."

"Item one: Six hundred dollars hotel rental."

"Six hundred dollars for how many days?"

"One. It's the hotel we're in now and the only room available was—"

"What's the name of this establishment?"

"The Hotel Romeo. It's a quiet place in the East Fifties, catering to wealthy honeymooners."

After a moment he requested, "Continue, please."

"Item two: Champagne breakfast . . . two hundred dollars."

"Who partook of that?"

"Nobody. It comes with the room and you have to take it. Did I tell you this is the Deluxe Cupid Suite? It is." She turned to the next page in the knee-resting notebook.

". . . Jimmy crack corn and I don't care . . ." drifted out of the bathroom, along with considerable scented steam.

"Item three: Room & board at the Sparkplug Country

Home in White Plains, New York . . . twelve hundred dollars.''

''I thought he was staying at the Romeo?''

''This is for the horse. She suffered a severe asthma attack and has to rest up for at least—''

''Never mind. Skip along to the next item. I assume there are more items.''

''Only two. Item four: Two hundred Little Dancing Men . . . three hundred fifty dollars. That's the wholesale price, by the way.''

Y hesitated before saying, ''Explain.''

''A fellow was selling them on the corner of Fifth Avenue and Fifty-third,'' she said. ''He had dozens of them tap dancing on the sidewalk when our runaway carriage jumped the curb and—''

''I see. And the final item?''

''Item five: One totem pole . . . seven hundred fifty dollars. That was out in front of the Canadian Royal Mounted Airways offices when we chanced to—''

''Fine. Send me the bills. Is there more?''

''No. They aren't going to bill us for the top hat or the buggy whip, so that's the lot, sir.''

''Tell Seven to report to me just as soon as he returns from his meeting with the CIA bloke.''

''Yes, I shall.''

''And don't compromise yourself.''

''I shan't.'' She hung up.

''As I walked out in the streets of Laredo,'' sang Seven.

Adjusting the fresh carnation in the lapel of his conservative gray business suit, Seven stepped through the glistening glass doors of the Marschall Gallery on Madison Avenue. A discreetly lettered placard stood on a plain wood easel just inside the entrance—*Food-inspired Sculpture: The Work of Elton Dornik.*

Seven ignored the catalog, sold by a slim blond Chinese girl seated at a small dead white table.

He halted in front of a six-foot-high ham sandwich on rye and pretended to be studying it. Actually he was paying no attention to the painted plaster sandwich replica and was studying the scatter of gallery patrons.

Two frail elderly ladies in fur coats were slowly circling a giant slice of cheesecake that towered over them. A trio of Japanese tourists was photographing the pizza that covered one wall of the gallery. Over near an immense bowl of oatmeal stood Bubber Kapusky, a broad, husky man without a hair on his head. Clad in a maroon leisure suit, the CIA agent was glancing from his catalog to the sculpture.

"What do you think?" he asked when Seven reached him. "Is it worth it?"

"What's the price?"

"Just forty-six thousand dollars." Kapusky rolled up the slim catalog, whapped himself on the thigh with it a few times. "I'm wondering if these things'll appreciate over, say, the next ten years."

"Oatmeal's been popular for centuries, running gruel a close second."

Kapusky began a slow, thoughtful circuit of the vast plaster bowl. "I'm also quite taken with the salami," he confided, squatting momentarily to inspect the underside of the bowl. "But I don't think they'd let me keep a seventeen-foot-long salami in my office, and unless I can display what I purchase in my office for at least a while, I can't write the damn thing off as a business expense."

"Can we have our talk here?"

"Yes, it's safe. I had one of my men sweep the joint for bugs," said the big CIA agent. "Found one in the ladies' room, but that was planted by the owner—he's a voyeur."

Seven sat on a plain wood bench that afforded him a view of an enormous chocolate chip cookie. "Are you CIA chaps on the trail of Underfoot?"

"Forty-six thousand dollars," muttered Kapusky, sitting next to him. "I'm really tempted. What's that you were asking, Seven?"

"Underfoot. Are you trying to—"

"We are, yes. It's important we find the man as soon as possible," he said. "We're also keeping a close watch on the increasing outbreaks of acute horniness here and abroad."

"Do you know how they deliver doses of the stuff?"

"Not as yet, although we hope to have—"

"I've been instructed by my superiors to cooperate with you," Seven told him. "Therefore, I can tell you that they may be using spray cans. I believe these cans are disguised as deodorant containers for a product called *Pitstop*!"

"That's clever. We didn't know that."

"One of my colleagues, at great personal risk to herself, has learned that the next test of the mist will take place in Southern California on Monday."

"Southern California is big. Where exactly?"

"We don't as yet know."

Kapusky said, "I have a piece of info for you, Seven. A nasty lady named Fancy Hooker has been hired to—"

"I know all about her. But it's my understanding she's been put on the sidelines."

"My info is that she got out of that steamer trunk you people had her stashed in and that she's en route here to terminate you."

Seven nodded. "Steamer trunks are relatively easy for a clever operative to get out of," he said. "Well, if Miss Hooker is on my scent again, I'd best be on my toes."

"We'll investigate this Los Angeles tip." Kapusky stood. "If we come up with anything, we'll let you know. Will you be heading West?"

"If that's the direction Los Angeles lies, yes." He stood.

"What do you think about the bowl of oatmeal?"

"I'd hold out for the salami." Seven headed for the exit.

Chapter 21

LOS ANGELES

The floor of the hotel suite shook slightly as B.J. paced. He jerked the sliding glass door of the balcony open, stomped out. "What's this crap?" he inquired, glaring, searching for a view.

"Smog," replied Dr. Maybe, joining him and gazing into the brown haze that surrounded them.

"Correct me if I'm wrong," snarled the large black man, "but aren't we residing at the Seaview Hotel?"

"This is the place, yes it is."

"I can't see the goddamn sea."

"If you squint your eyes and lean to the left, like I'm doing, you can almost make out something that just might be the Pacific Ocean over yonder," said the Oriental, pointing.

"For three hundred dollars a day I don't want to have to guess at the view."

Maybe was looking back into the hotel room, a bit anxiously. ''Look on the bright side,'' he suggested. ''This thick blanket of eye-blighting miasma will cover our activities. Make it much more difficult for our enemies and antagonists to—''

''Why do you keep eyeing the living room?''

''Well, Dr. Yes rang for room service a few minutes ago and I want to make sure he doesn't eat the waiter.''

''For three hundred dollars a day they can throw in a waiter or two.'' B.J. thumped down into a canvas deck chair, scowling out at the Southern California beach town that was probably out there somewhere. ''I'm not at all pleased with the way things are going.''

''What things?''

''To name but one—Fancy Hooker. You assholes assured me she'd punch Triple 'O' Seven's ticket with ease,'' he said. ''Instead she gets dumped in a trunk and—''

''She got out.''

''She lets some skinny, flat-chested Limey agent put her in a trunk and—''

''Fancy escaped B.J. She's back in Manhattan even as we speak, planning a new and better way to get rid of Seven.''

''He'll probably pack her in a piano crate.'' Jobb stood up, cracking his knuckles angrily. ''Once, not that long ago, it was only the British we had to worry about. Now we got the goddamn CIA, we got this T. Texas Bedrock who's trying to steal our formula. I hear the Vatican is down on us. Things, Dr. Maybe, are not running smoothly.''

''That's the nature of this line of work. My late father,

for instance, had problems when he went up against Triple 'O' Seven's dad."

B.J. asked, "Are we all set for Monday?"

"All is in readiness."

Returning to the living room, B.J. noticed a wheeled serving cart with a silver-covered dish atop it. "Dr. Yes?"

From the bedroom came a muffled response. "You called?"

"Get your butt in here."

The Oriental came trotting in, picking at his teeth with a matchstick. "You wanted me?"

Jobb jabbed a finger in the direction of the serving cart. "Where's the waiter who goes with this?"

"Been here and gone." He smiled blandly, spread his hands wide. "He delivered my BLT, sneered at my generous tip, and took his leave."

B.J. resumed pacing. "We have our biggest test coming up on Monday," he reminded them. "If the Underfoot formula works as well here as it has elsewhere, then we can start using it in every major city in the Western World. In a many of weeks civilization will grind to a halt and we'll move in to take over."

"When you say 'we'," said Dr. Yes, "you mean Russia, I take it."

"Perhaps."

Dr. Maybe said, "You're not intending to cross the KGB? They can get awfully mean if—"

"Right now let's just concentrate on Monday."

"They can do all sorts of painful things to you."

"I do painful things to people, too. So keep in mind

that . . . What are these?'' He stooped, grabbed up a pair of black shoes from under the coffee table.

Dr. Yes scrutinized them. ''Pair of shoes would be my guess.''

''Waiter shoes,'' accused B.J. in a booming voice, waving them.

Dr. Maybe sighed. ''You promised not to snack on the help while we—''

''Do I look like a glutton? How could I eat an entire waiter in just a few minutes?''

''Are these his shoes?'' said Jobb.

''Well, yes,'' admitted Dr. Yes, with a bored shrug. ''But he simply jumped out of them.''

''Why?''

''Merely because he misconstrued my innocent observation that he looked very much like a plum pudding.''

''Oh, you didn't frighten Rudy, did you?'' asked Dr. Maybe, uneasy.

''Didn't catch his name.''

''Rudy's an awfully charming young man, and he does somewhat resemble a plum pudding. I've sort of had my eye on him since we checked—''

''Enough,'' suggested B.J. He dropped the shoes. ''Get out our maps, Dr. Maybe, and let's go over our plans once more.''

Chapter 22

NEW YORK

The Los Angeles-bound airliner had been in the air less than fifteen minutes when Emily leaned close to Triple 'O' Seven and whispered, "Have you noticed anything odd or unusual about the other passengers on our flight?"

He had the window seat and was gazing out into the twilight, watching the lights of the great metropolis grow smaller and smaller. "They're not," he replied, "an especially lively lot."

"Anything else?"

Seven turned away from the window. "Quite a few of them look a great deal alike," he said. "I assume we've found ourselves in the midst of a family excursion."

"All the women are young, beautiful, and well dressed. All the men are young, handsome, and well dressed."

"Now that you mention it, Emily, that is decidedly unusual."

"I've been very subtly scanning them," she told him, still speaking in a whisper. "Each and every one of them sits stiff and still, staring straight ahead."

"Strange, since the attendants haven't passed out the complimentary drinks yet."

Emily took hold of his arm. "I'm very much afraid, Trip, that we've walked into a trap."

"You think so? Merely because we seem to be sharing our westward flight with a planeload of conservative yuppies?"

Her grip on his upper arm tightened. "They're all dummies, department store mannequins."

Very casually he glanced across the aisle. "That chap over there does look rather dummylike," he concluded. "Though vaguely familiar."

"You've probably seen him in the window of Bloomingdale's."

Nodding, the mustached agent said, "Buying up several dozen department store dummies, outfitting them in smart clothes, and filling a jet airplane with them is an expensive and time-consuming task. That means we're dealing with the KGB yet again."

"And quite probably with this B. Jobb, who is their minion and toady."

Drumming his fingers on the armrest, Seven said, "I've been a goose. I should have been much more observant and spotted this ruse while we were much closer to the ground."

"So should I have, Trip." She shook her head sadly. "This only confirms P's feeling that agents of the opposite sex should avoid growing too fond of each other and thus pay more attention to each other than to matters more important."

Seven grinned. "I'm glad to hear that you're fond enough of me to—"

"To neglect my duty." She shook her head again. "Well, enough sentimental gush. Let's figure out how to extricate ourselves from this mess."

"Certainly we're in a pickle." He took another look around the cabin. "Yes, dummies all. And, now that I notice, there is not a single flight attendant aboard. They must've jumped ship before we took off."

"That explains why no one gave us the usual welcoming speech or explained how to use our oxygen masks."

He patted her hand. "I'm going to make my way discreetly to the pilots' cabin, and—"

"Welcome aboard Flight 104 for oblivion, chumps," came a harsh feminine voice out of the overhead speakers. "This is your pilot speaking."

"I recognize that voice," whispered Emily. "It's Fancy Hooker."

"That makes sense. I was warned by that CIA fellow that she was on the loose again, and bent on—"

"The green stuff you see gushing out of the air vents," announced Fancy Hooker, "is a special knockout gas. In sixty seconds or less you dimwits'll be in the land of snooze."

"Not if I can . . ." Seven made an effort to leave his seat.

Instead he slumped and fell asleep.

He opened his eyes. He found he was staring into something gray and fuzzy.

He felt the gray and fuzzy stuff with his hand.

"Feels a good deal like carpeting," he observed.

After making a few more tests and calculations, he concluded he was stretched out, facedown, on a patch of gray carpeting.

There was a drone and the feeling of motion.

"Might I be," he asked himself, "flat out in the aisle of our airliner?"

He pushed at the floor, got himself to a crouching position, and looked around.

"Yes, that's it."

Seven had been sprawled in the aisle, unconscious.

After resting for a moment, he grabbed the arm of the nearest seat and pulled himself upright.

He didn't feel particularly dizzy or unstable.

"This KGB knockout gas doesn't leave one with the hangover the brand Bitchy Sue and her papa used on me."

He remembered Emily then and turned toward the seat they'd been sharing.

The young woman wasn't there.

Zzzzzznnnn.

"What's that noise?"

Zzzzzzznnnnnn.

It was a faint humming, wheezing sound, coming from somewhere in the cabin.

"Someone snoring, that's what it is."

He started moving forward along the aisle toward the pilots' cabin.

Zzzzzzzznnnnnnn.

He was getting closer to whoever it was who was snoring.

"Is that you, Emily? How'd you get way up here?"

The snoring person was in the first-class section of the

airliner, next to a handsome young dummy in a natty blue suit.

But the sleeper was not Emily.

It was a dark-haired woman dressed in an airplane pilot's uniform. She was slouched far to the right in the aisle seat, left arm dangling.

"By George, this is Fancy Hooker," realized Seven. "Yes, I recognize her from the dossier photos I've seen. She's, I must say, a bit more weather-beaten than she appeared in her photographs."

He straightened up, frowning. "If she's out cold, who's piloting this plane?"

The door of the pilots' cabin opened.

"Do you have any bumps or bruises?" asked Emily, looking at him with concern.

He examined himself. "Nothing much. Should I?"

"Well, I sort of threw you at Fancy," she explained. "Don't be angry, since you were the only thing handy and I didn't dare go for my gun. I was feigning unconsciousness and, when I realized that you were truly out, I decided on the spur of the moment to make use of you as a battering ram of sorts. You served quite well for knocking Fancy completely off her pins. I was then able to—"

"How did you come to be feigning unconsciousness? Didn't that gas—"

"I thought Z had fitted you with one of these new nose gas masks," she said, tapping the side of her pretty nose. "It seems everyone has one but I."

"I'm sorry I left you in the aisle, but I had to make certain our plane wouldn't crash," she said. "After that I had to interrogate Fancy and what with one thing and another, I'm just now getting around to coming back to see how you are."

"I'm as well as can be expected." He nodded at the slumbering Fancy. "What did you use on her?"

"Something new Z gave me, comes concealed in a candy dispenser. It's both a truth drug and a sleeping potion."

"What did you learn?"

Emily smiled, pleased with herself. "I know exactly where they're going to run their next test."

"That's splendid. Where?"

She said, "I've got the plane on automatic and we won't be arriving over Los Angeles for another hour and a half, Trip. Why don't we talk later."

"Doing what in the meantime?"

Coming up close, she put her arms around him.

Chapter 23

LOS ANGELES

Halfway across the vast glass-walled lobby Seven halted. "Explain this place to me again, Emily," he requested of the young blond woman at his side.

"We're at the Ziggyland Hotel, which rises up in the heart of the world-famous Ziggyland amusement park that covers multiple acres here in Southern California."

"I understand that, and that it's all named after some cartoonist chap, now deceased, named Bud Ziggy."

Emily said, "Fancy Hooker told me, while under the influence of the truth drug, that B.J. and his cohorts will test the gas here at Ziggyland someplace on Monday."

"I understand that," he said. "But what I'm not clear on is why our bellhop is dressed like a rat and the registration clerk is got up to resemble a duck."

"All the bellhops dress like Ronny Rat," she explained

as she took his arm and started him moving again. "The clerks are wearing Buck Duck costumes."

"Oh, so?"

"Ronny Rat and Buck Duck are well-known animated cartoon characters. The Bud Ziggy fortunes were built on their success."

Nodding, Seven allowed himself to be led by her up to the desk. "I never cared for cartoons as a child," he said.

"Neither did I," said the clerk with the duck head, having overheard him. "And look where I end up. That's irony for you." He slid across a registration card. "Study to be a concert pianist and end up here. Okay, I studied by correspondence course, but I still think it's a fall from greatness. My mother agrees."

"You're still in touch?"

"That's her running the newsstand over there, dressed up like Lizzie Pig."

Emily said, "I want to pick up a few magazines, Trip. Be back in a moment."

"Yes, I was a child prodigy," continued the clerk, scratching at the feathers on his scalp. "The Boy Wonder of the Keyboard I was called. Well, mostly it was my mother and my Aunt Marie who called me that, but even so."

"Exactly," said Seven, returning the form.

The clerk glanced at it and then turned to the computer terminal beside him. "Ah yes, Mr. and Mrs. Wally Reisberson of Albany, California. You're in . . . yes, Suite 1313. That's on our thirteenth floor. I do hope you're not superstitious."

"Not a bit."

"I am. Fact of the matter is, I got stuck on this low rung of life's ladder of success because I broke a mirror some three years back."

Emily returned carrying two fashion magazines and a large stuffed Ronny Rat. "Isn't this charming?"

"Not especially. Did you buy that thing?"

"No, the lady running the stand gave it to me," she explained as they started for the elevators in the wake of their bellhop. "I'm the one millionth customer and therefore entitled to a free stuffed toy."

"You really think that thing is attractive?" inquired their bellhop, punching the button for thirteen.

"Yes, don't you?"

He tapped the Ronny Rat head he was wearing. "Underneath this I'm a dead ringer for Warner Baxter. Yet I go around day in and day out looking like a rodent."

"Who's Warner Baxter?" asked Seven politely.

"That's another burden I have to live with. I resemble a handsome movie actor of the nineteen thirties that only a dwindling handful of old coots remember at all," he complained. "I couldn't look like Burt Reynolds or Wayne Newton or some other dashing celebrity with a mustache. Oh, no, not me. Here's our floor."

He led them down a wide hall that was carpeted with a rug containing likenesses of all the major Bud Ziggy characters. He stowed their luggage, introduced them to the suite, and, accepting a tip, departed.

Emily said, "I believe I'll take a shower."

Seven snapped his fingers. "That reminds me."

"Of what?"

He looked down at the carpet, also rich with Ziggy

characters. "Oh, I have to purchase a certain . . . um . . . rather intimate product." He edged toward the door. "I'll pop down to the lobby and return in a jiffy."

Emily smiled, setting her free Ronny Rat on the bedside table. "I'll look forward to your return," she said.

Seven leaned across the newsstand counter and asked, in a low voice, "I beg pardon, ma'am, but do you have any of these . . . um . . . contraceptives that don't have Bud Ziggy characters on them?"

The plump woman on the other side of the counter was slumped in a folding chair. She wasn't wearing her Lizzie Pig head.

"In fact, she appears to be out cold." Deftly, he leapt over the counter.

The costume head was lying on the floor. He stepped around it, took hold of the woman's wrist.

"Ma'am, what's wrong here?"

". . . drugged . . . shot in arm . . . took my place . . ."

He let go of her. "Then the person who waited on Emily a few moments ago was an imposter," he realized. "She wasn't the millionth customer. And she was given that Ronny Rat doll for some more sinister purpose."

Leaping back over the counter, Seven dashed toward the house telephones.

All three were occupied.

The chunky man nearest to Seven was saying, "On the other hand, Irene, with the thirty-two-dollar Ziggyland ticket book we get all that plus the cruise on the pirate ship, a ride on the Death Mountain roller coaster, two meals at the Old-Fashioned Rat Café, and six—"

"Pardon me, sir, but this is something of an emergency."

The man scowled at him, his sunburned forehead wrinkling. "Go piss up a rope, buddy. Nothing, hon. Six complete rides on the mammoth Ziggyland merry-go-round, a trip to the moon in the Jules Verne rocket, plus . . . unk!"

The impatient Seven had dealt him an incapacitating blow to the kidneys.

As the man fell, Seven caught the receiver from his hand. He broke the connection, then dialed 1313.

The phone in their room rang five times, and another five.

"Damn, she's still in the shower. And I can't warn her."

He waited for five more rings and then sprinted toward the elevators.

A thick-set man in a dog suit was hanging up a sign that announced—*Elevators Temporarily Out of Order. The Ziggyland Hotel Apologizes for Any Inconvenience.*

"Out of order?" said Seven.

"That's what the sign says," said the dog.

"How soon will you have them fixed?"

"It's not my department, but I'd estimate an hour. It should only take a half hour, but the repair crew has to wear Dummy Bunny costumes and it's tough to handle tools with furry little paws."

"I can't wait." Seven ran to the stairway, yanked open the fire door, and started upward. "There may be a bomb in that stuffed toy. Or worse."

* * *

He paused for an instant on the tenth floor to catch his breath.

Then he continued bounding up the stairs, three steps at a time.

"Perhaps it's not a bomb," he told himself as he swiftly climbed higher. "Might be they merely planted a listening device. It could even be an innocent Ronny Rat toy, although one would hardly go to the trouble of drugging that innocent lady to pass Emily a free toy."

He reached the eleventh floor.

The twelfth.

The thirteenth.

The door was stuck, wouldn't budge.

Seven twisted the knob, pushed hard with his shoulder.

This time, creaking, it opened and he was in the corridor.

He ran along the decorative carpeting, dodged a maid's cart, and reached the door of 1313.

"Damn, I didn't bother to take my key," he realized.

He banged on the door. "Emily, quick! Open up!"

There was no response.

"Emily! It's urgent!"

A maid looked out of an open doorway across the way. "Is something wrong, sir?"

"Passkey. Do you have one?"

"Well, yes, I do. But if you and your missus had a fight and she locked you out, I don't think I ought to—"

"No, actually she's subject to fainting spells. I'm afraid she may have passed out in there."

"Well, in that case I suppose—"

"Yes, splendid." He bolted over to her, grabbed the

key she was taking from the pocket of her uniform. Back at the door, he inserted the key, turned, and dived inside.

"Emily?"

He could hear the shower running in the bathroom.

Ronny Rat was still sprawled on the bedside table.

"No time to disarm him."

Seven lifted up the toy by its floppy ears, ran over to the balcony door and took hold of the handle on the sliding glass panel.

It didn't open.

"You can't open them at all, sir," said the maid from the hallway. "On account of children might fall and grown-ups commit suicide."

Seven picked up a heavy chair and started banging at the glass.

Six swats were sufficient to smash through.

"You oughtn't to do that," called the maid.

He thrust the toy under his arm like a football and stepped out onto the narrow little balcony.

The street below was thick with cars and pedestrians.

But beyond it stretched a wide lagoon that was empty save for a pair of swans.

"I'm fond of swans," he said, "yet I have no choice."

He took aim, calculated the distance, and lobbed the Ronny Rat out over the balcony railing.

It sailed cleanly over the busy roadway, splashed into the lagoon.

Roughly eight seconds passed and then there was an enormous whomping explosion followed by an impressive geyser of water, mixed with steam and white feathers.

"So it wasn't just a listening device." He stepped back

into the living room, crossed, and shut the door on the astonished maid.

Emily, wearing nothing but a towel, stepped in from the bathroom. ''Did I miss something?''

''Fortunately, yes,'' he replied.

Chapter 24

Bubber Kapusky tripped over something as he made his way across the immense dark lawn of the presidential ranch in Southern California. "Oops," he said, recognizing what he'd stumbled over as he got to his feet. "Excuse me, Mr. Secretary."

The secretary of state murmured, "Think nothing of it, m'boy." He smiled amiably up at the CIA agent and the clear, star-filled sky overhead, then dozed off.

Kapusky continued on toward the large, ranch-style house, where lights were showing in several of the rooms.

Before he reached his destination a figure emerged from the house. "Have you seen him?" asked Wally Watergate.

"The secretary of state, you mean?" The CIA agent pointed in the direction he'd come. "He's sleeping it off about two hundred feet down—"

"I know about him. I'm looking for President Sandcastle."

"Haven't seen him."

Watergate thrust his hands into the pockets of his slacks. "I should've known better than to trust him alone," he said. "But he swore he was just coming down to greet your helicopter."

"He didn't show up there. Have you tried the stable?"

"That's right, he does wander in there sometimes." He started walking in that direction and Kapusky tagged along. "I think I'm beginning to lose heart, Bubber. The minute he appointed a man named Harry 'Woo Woo' Gernsbacker to be secretary of state, I knew we were starting on a downhill phase. Now he's got the notion it's possible to run for a third term."

"What term does he think he's serving now?"

"He knows this is his second one—he's still fairly sharp in some ways. But lately he's been talking a lot about how Roosevelt served four terms and he'd like to break that record."

"I have to fill him in on the Underfoot situation."

"What's going on there anyway? I understand that British guy we're supposed to be working with blew up the Ziggyland Hotel this afternoon."

"Where'd you hear that?"

"It was on the six o'clock news."

"You ought to know by now that the media tends to exaggerate," said Kapusky. "Triple 'O' Seven simply tossed a bomb out the window of his hotel suite and into a nearby lagoon."

"In the habit of throwing bombs out of windows for the fun of it, is he? I know Secretary of State Gernsbacker is fond of firecrackers and—"

"The bomb had been planted in his room. If he hadn't

thrown it out the window, several people would have been killed."

"He's the same guy who lost a battleship, isn't he?"

"I think it was an airplane he lost."

Watergate paused at the entrance to the shadowy stable building. "Mr. President? Are you in there?"

After a moment came, "Is that you, Willis?"

"Close, sir. It's Wally."

"You'll do. Come on in, Wally."

"You know Bubber Kapusky, sir."

"Do I?"

Watergate located a light switch and flipped it. The lane between the empty stalls was illuminated and there was the president of the United States sitting on a bale of hay, dressed in jeans and a plaid shirt.

"I'm with the CIA, Mr. President."

"Oh yes, I recall now. And how are things with the CIA?"

"We've been rather concerned about this Underfoot affair and our promise to work closely with the British," he said. "It's been decided that we want sole credit for capturing this B. Jobb and his associates on Monday. Therefore we'll pretend to continue cooperating with Triple 'O' Seven, but actually we've arranged for him to be kept out of action for the entire day."

"That's a sound plan."

"Thank you, sir."

"Sure, I did something like that in *Two Gun Kid from Tijuana* in 1926. Only instead of the Brih it was the greasers . . . excuse me, the Chicanos that I flummoxed." He inhaled, looked up at Watergate. "What was the name of that fellow who wore the white hat and rode the white horse?''

''The Lone Ranger?''

''No, this was in the silents.''

''Warner Baxter,'' suggested Kapusky.

President Sandcastle shook his head. ''He didn't have a mustache, this fellow. Wore a cowboy-style tuxedo, with fringe, to Hollywood parties.''

''Tom Mix?'' guessed Watergate.

''Tom Mix.'' The president nodded. ''That's who I was trying to think of, yes. Haven't seen him in ages. Well . . .'' He pushed at his knees and slowly rose into a standing position. ''What exactly am I doing out here at this time of night, Wallace?''

''You came out to meet Bubber.''

''Well, then I've taken care of that and I can turn in, can't I?'' Chuckling, he started for the doorway.

Chapter 25

It was a warm clear Sunday afternoon and the brightly painted paddlewheel steamboat was chuffing its way slowly along a very convincing stretch of wide muddy river.

"We hope all you folks are enjoying," said a voice over the public address system, "this showboat cruise along the picturesque Mrs. Ziggy River. Just one of the many wondrous attractions . . ."

On the upper deck, in a patch of sunlight, Emily and Seven were seated at one of the small white café tables. "I think doing what they suggest is foolish," Seven was saying.

Emily, wearing a simple blue summer dress, had a small tan attaché case resting on the table top next to her root beer mug. "Since we're cooperating with the CIA on this whole operation, Trip, we pretty much have to go along with Agent Kapusky's suggestions and plans."

"What's he dressing up as?"

She consulted her notebook. "Dirty Dog."

"That sounds like a bit more fun than my being Ronny Rat."

"Ronny Rat is, after all, the star Bud Ziggy animated character. So that your dressing up as him makes you—"

"Look like a bloody fool." He slouched in his chair. "What costume do they want you to wear?"

"I'm to be Fanny Rat," she answered. "Ronny's lady friend."

"We'll make quite a couple."

"We shall," she agreed, smiling across at him. "You must admit that dressing up as Ziggy characters tomorrow will allow us to prowl the entire park without attracting attention. There are dozens of employees already dressed as the major characters and—"

"I envision tourists asking me to pose for photographs with their ill-mannered offspring."

"Be that as it may, it's good cover."

He drummed his fingertips on the side of his lemonade glass and glanced at the riverbank, where a scatter of very convincing robots were supposed to be black dockworkers carrying bales of cotton. "Have our own people learned anything further?"

"I was about to check with our local branch." She unlocked the attaché case, using a key that hung on a golden chain around her neck.

"What's in the case?"

"A compact computer terminal. Z's invention."

"All he put in my attaché case was a bicycle," remarked Seven. "Three-speed at that."

She had the case open and was using the keyboard. "I'll see what—"

"Ought you to be using that gadget so openly?"

"Trip, we're in Southern California, where just about everybody is a workaholic," she told him. "Seeing someone fooling with a briefcase or a portable computer during a weekend outing isn't at all unusual."

"Seems a bit gauche, as well as risky."

She concentrated on the terminal. "Our people have learned," she said after a moment of reading information off the screen, "that alleged representatives of the so-called *Pitstop*! company have obtained permission to distribute two hundred thousand sample cans of their deodorant here on the Ziggyland grounds tomorrow."

He asked, "Where are these two hundred thousand cans at the moment?"

"No information on that as yet, but it's being looked into," Emily replied. "Here's something that might be of interest. The local police suspect, judging from remains found in a trash bin behind the Ziggyland Outskirts Ritz Hotel, that one of the hotel's room service waiters was the victim of a cannibal."

Seven sat up in his cane-bottom chair. "By George, that sounds like a chap named Dr. Yes."

"So our people felt. A person answering Dr. Yes's description was registered at the hotel but checked out just before the body was found."

"He's both a cannibal and a glutton. I remember he once tried to go on a diet and eat only midgets, but—"

"Didn't your father and his father—"

"They were antagonists some years ago," he acknowledged. "There seem to be quite a few second-generation scoundrels involved in this Underfoot affair."

"Many people seem compelled to carry on the family business."

"I'm not at all certain that I'm one of them."

"Don't look so glum." She shut the case, placed it on the deck, and reached across to take his hand. "You've done a splendid job thus far."

"Would that I could agree with you." He stared gloomily out across the waters of the imitation river. "I was rather taken aback this morning when that delegation from the Southern California Friends of Our Feathered Friends came round to our new suite to accuse me of being a swan-killer."

"It was, after all, merely two swans you killed, and that was by accident."

"Apparently that was enough to enrage them."

"My feeling is, it's better to kill swans than people."

"My attitude exactly," he said, grinning at her. "I must say, Emily, you're proving to be a very sensible person."

Late that same afternoon Bubber Kapusky was to be seen walking along a fashionable street of shops in the vicinity of Beverly Hills. He took a small notebook from the pocket of his gray suit coat and consulted it. "Name of the place is Mother Scum's Greasy Spoon," he confirmed. "Ought to be just about . . . Yep, there it is."

The narrow restaurant was wedged between a boutique called Sloppy Joe's, which had a single pair of faded, wrinkled jeans thrown over a wooden sawhorse in its display window, and a jewelry shop named Mr. Outrageous.

Mother Scum's Greasy Spoon had been designed to look like a cheap café of several decades ago. It had a dirty glass window with its name lettered on it in peeling white paint, faded and tattered strawberry café curtains, and a dangling strip of overpopulated flypaper.

The husky CIA agent was reaching for the doorknob when a huge black man stepped out of the shadows to grab him by the sleeve.

"Where you think you going, mother?"

"Inside, and I'd advise you to—"

"Inside? You think, peckerhead, you just going to go waltzing in to Mother Scum's and sit down?"

"That was my intention unless—"

"You got an invitation, Jim?"

."Oh, you're the maître d'," realized Kapusky. "I thought for a minute I was being mugged."

"I asked you a question, putz."

"I'm meeting someone and I assume she's got a reservation."

"What's her frigging name?"

"Pam Sitcominsky."

The larger man shook his head. "Never heard of her. Take a hike."

"You've memorized the reservations list?"

"For the next six weeks, buttwipe."

The CIA agent refrained from reaching inside his coat for his Charter Arms Bulldog revolver. Shooting down this oaf would only complicate his meeting with the local agent. "She may have made the reservation under her professional name," he said. "Miss South Dakota of 1979."

"You should of said that in the first damn place,

schmuck.'' He opened the smudged wooden door, gave the CIA man a vigorous shove. ''Get your ass on in to Booth thirteen, be quick about it, too.''

The restaurant was small, crowded, and full of noise. There were about fifteen rickety green booths along one wall, a battered counter along the other. The smell of burned cooking fat and fried onions dominated the humid air and an authentic-looking old jukebox against the back wall was roaring out an ancient rock tune.

From Booth 13 emerged a tan hand to wave at him. ''Hurry up, Bubber, or they'll toss me out.''

''Geeze, buddy,'' said the waiter, who was standing, arms folded, next to the booth, ''don't youse got no idea what time it is?''

''I'm only four minutes late for—''

''Five minutes late and the booth goes to the next on the list.''

Kapusky slid in opposite the busty redhead he'd come here to meet. ''Good afternoon, Pam. It's nice to—''

''Gab later,'' advised their waiter. ''Order first.'' He was a squat man of about forty, wearing an undershirt, tan slacks, tennis shoes, and no socks. His long white apron was spattered with grease and blood.

The menu was a grease-stained mimeographed sheet of paper. ''Well, let's see what you have to offer on—''

''I ain't got all flapping day.''

Kapusky resisted the impulse to pull his gun and shoot him. ''Let's see. 'Hamburger . . . twenty-five dollars. With pickle and lettuce . . . thirty dollars. On a bun . . . thirty-five dollars.' '' He looked across at Pam Sitcominsky. ''What're you having?''

''The baloney sandwich.''

He found that on the wrinkled menu. " 'Baloney Sandwich . . . forty dollars.' Nope, that's not for me. I'll just have a cup of coffee—at five dollars—and a doughnut—at eight dollars."

"Read the fine print at the bottom, jerko." The waiter scratched at his armpit, then leaned in and pointed at the menu.

" 'Minimum charge per person . . . twenty-five dollars.' Okay, I'll have coffee, two doughnuts, and Jell-O."

"We ran out of Jell-O."

"What are you offering instead?"

"Nothing."

"Three doughnuts then."

"About time. Do youse want a glass of water?"

"On the house?"

"Fat chance. It's a buck."

"I'll pass."

"Some big spender you hooked up with, honey." The waiter departed.

"Why this place?" Kapusky asked Pam.

"It's new and trendy," she answered. "I've been anxious to try it. Usually you have to wait weeks to get a reservation, but a friend of mine swapped her reservation for mine at Harpoon Louie's Cafeteria, which is the new chic spot in Malibu. Besides which, Bubber, there's so much noise here no one can hear what we say to each other."

"I've made all the arrangements," he informed her. "You'll report to Ziggyland tomorrow morning at eight and be sworn in as a Ziggyland Guide. I'm wondering, though . . ."

"About what?"

"You may be a bit too zaftig to pass as an innocent college girl working her way—"

"Hey, only a few years ago I was a sweet innocent college girl," she reminded him. "Then fate took a hand and I became Miss South Dakota."

"Could you wear something less form-fitting tomorrow?"

"Lots of sweet, innocent girls have big tits, Bubber."

"True, but I don't want you to draw undue attention," he told her. "You have to come across as relatively demure."

"I can fake demure."

"All right. Soon as you get into your Guide outfit, you call on Seven and his associate, Emily Watts-Batsfree, and tell them you're a CIA agent assigned—"

"I actually am a CIA agent. Don't you want me to lie to—"

"Seven will be expecting you," said Kapusky. "You're going to escort them, so he thinks, to my command post for the day. But you'll explain to them that, since they're wearing Ziggy character costumes as disguises, that they have to circulate in the park a bit in order to divert suspicion. Then you take them to the Death Mountain roller coaster and get them into a couple of seats. Just as it's about to take off, you pretend to have forgotten something and you step off. It's been arranged for the roller coaster to stall at its highest point. It ought to take Seven, even if he decides to hoof it, a couple of hours to get down."

A disappointed pout touched her face. "This doesn't sound like Anglo-American teamwork to me, Bubber."

"It isn't. We want Seven on the sidelines while we

move in and capture these Russian-backed agents ourselves."

"Good thing Winston Churchill isn't alive to—"

"Who had the baloney?" asked the returned waiter.

"I did," said Pam.

"This is it, sister. Ignore the damn footprints on your Wonder Bread. I dropped the plate and the stupid busboy walked across it with his brogans."

Chapter 26

The maid was sitting on the sofa, feet up on the coffee table, smoking a small cigar.

When Seven, stepping into their suite at the Ziggyland Hotel, saw her, he pushed Emily behind him and reached for his Baretta.

"Relax, Triple 'O' Seven," the maid said, swinging her feet off the glass-top table. "I'm from the local branch of Special Intelligence. You know me as V."

He took a few steps toward her, eyes narrowing as he studied the plump, gray-haired woman. "Why are you dressed in female garb?"

"Because I'm a female."

"Oh, good," said Emily. "Another triumph for feminists."

"Not so fast," cautioned Seven. "I'll have to ask you to identify yourself, V."

After snuffing out her cigar in the Ronny Rat ashtray,

she said, "twenty-three-eighteen-fifteen-twenty-five, twenty-eight-nine-nineteen."

He let his gun hand drop to his side. "Yes, that's correct."

"Why are you got up as a maid?" Emily came into their living room and sat in an armchair facing the local SI chief.

"Simplest way to get around this hotel unobserved, dear."

"And why," asked Seven, "was it necessary to drop in on us, V?"

She said, "We've come up with some rather important information that I wanted you two to have at once. Besides, I had to come here anyway to take a look at the damage you two did to 1313." She pointed at the ceiling with her thumb.

"It was I who did all the damage," volunteered Seven, leaning against the wall and folding his arms.

From the bosom of her maid's uniform V withdrew a rolled sheet of thin paper. "Let's turn to matters more important than a ruined bathtub now, and—"

"I never ruined any bathtub," protested Seven. "When we vacated 1313, the tub was in pristine—"

"Not important, Seven. SI will pay the thirty-five hundred dollars for it and—"

"One would think that a hotel named after a man who devoted his entire life to bringing decent, wholesome entertainment to millions of innocent children wouldn't pad the bill for damages to—"

"Allow her to continue, Trip."

"Very well. Excuse me." He unfolded his arms, bowed

toward V, refolded them. "Thirty-five hundred dollars for a bathtub seems ridiculous, but let it pass."

V unfurled the paper, which turned out to be a complex and detailed floor plan. "This is the layout of the underground facilities here at Ziggyland," she explained, tapping it. "As you may know, there are business offices, storerooms, costume warehouses, and repair shops beneath the park itself."

Emily leaned forward in her chair. "You've learned of something else that's down there?"

"We have, dear. In this room here—labeled Storeroom eight—there are two hundred thousand containers of *Pitstop*!"

"Excellent bit of intelligence work," said Seven. "I suggest we get down there for a look-see, as soon as we notify the CIA of what we've learned. Or have you done that already?"

"We have not." V looked up at him. "And that brings me to another matter I must discuss. We have good reason to believe that Bubber Kapusky and his CIA associates intend not to honor their earlier agreement with SI."

"How so?"

"There is a plan afoot to sidetrack you and Emily tomorrow, making sure you're both out of the way until the Russian agents are safely captured and incapacitated."

"That's hardly," commented Seven, "sporting."

"It isn't, but keep in mind that this is America and not Great Britain."

Emily said, "If we were to explore that storeroom tonight, we might just be able to nab Jobb and his minions. We could do it before the CIA has a chance to sabotage us."

"Exactly what we think." V smiled at her. "Therefore I am instructing you and Triple 'O' Seven to get cracking."

"We shall."

"There are now six Special Intelligence agents in place around Ziggyland," continued V. "As soon as you've determined what the situation is below, you can contact them to move in and take over, if need be." She passed the floor plans across to Emily. "There is one other thing I must mention."

"Yes?" said Seven.

V cleared her throat. "It seems that the late Bud Ziggy was a great believer in applied technology," she said. "When he died a few years ago, he stipulated in his will that his body was to be kept here in Ziggyland, frozen. It was his wish that eventually a robot replica of him would be built and, once it was perfected, his brain was to be transferred to the mechanical simulacrum's head. As soon, that is, as science works out a way to bring a brain back to life."

"Immortality," said Emily.

"Of a sort, yes."

Seven frowned. "Why are you telling us this anecdote?"

"Simply because Ziggy's body and the lab that manufactures the many impressive robots you see about the park lies underground and quite close to Storeroom eight."

"Are you hinting that I might blunder into that lab by mistake?" asked Seven. "That I might cause damage, might upset Bud Ziggy's plans for reincarnation?"

"Special Intelligence feels," said V diplomatically, "that the man who could tip over a rather substantial replica of Notre Dame Cathedral in the course of an investigation, purely by accident though it was, ought to be cautioned to be careful while in the vicinity of a rather illustrious corpse and considerable valuable electronic equipment."

"In saving civilization from utter ruin," put in Emily angrily, "one sometimes has to take risks, V."

"No need to grow upset, dear." V stood. "A word to the wise will be, I'm sure, sufficient. I am confident that you two will carry things off tonight without a single snag."

"Of course," said Emily, smiling over at Seven.

He continued to scowl.

Seven's shoes made squishy sounds as he walked along the underground corridor. "I still think we could've found a less hazardous means of getting down here," he said.

"It wasn't hazardous," countered Emily. "And by coming down through the sewer conduits we avoided being spotted by any of the security—"

"I've been very fond of these shoes, and now they're fatally waterlogged."

"They look fine, Trip." She again consulted the floor plan V had provided them. "I'd estimate we're now about a mile from Storeroom eight."

"My socks didn't fare any too well either."

"I'll knit you a new pair," she promised, "once we're home again in England."

"That's very thoughtful of you."

They continued on along the gray-walled corridor, following its twists and turns.

"I think we're just about—"

"Quiet a second." He touched her arm.

"What?" she whispered.

He nodded his head in the direction they'd come. "Footfalls."

She hunched her shoulders slightly as she listened. "Yes, two people at least and coming our way."

"We'd best duck in here until they pass." He pointed at the nearest door.

It was labled *Robotics Lab #1 & Bud Ziggy Mausoleum*.

The sound of footsteps was growing louder.

"No, I don't think V would want us to hide in this particular—"

"Nonsense. There's no time to go on to the next doorway." He tried the handle. It turned and he eased the door open.

"You more or less promised that you—"

"Inside." He went in, pulling her with him and closing the door silently.

They found themselves in a large, high-ceilinged workshop. There were several long, gray metal worktables, each heavy with electronic equipment and an array of tools. Lined up against one wall were a dozen or more robots, most of them nearly complete.

"There's Mark Twain," recognized Emily. "And Blackbeard the Pirate."

"And Queen Victoria."

"Next to her is . . . oh, my."

"What's wrong?"

She shuddered, pointing to a faintly lit alcove across the room. "That must be . . . *him*."

There was a body resting atop a low, flat, marble slab and covered by a dome of incredibly clear glass. The corpse was a man of about sixty-five, tall and mustached, dressed in nubby tan slacks and a tweedy sport coat with leather patches on the elbows.

Seven said, "Yes, that must indeed be Bud Ziggy and—"

"Don't go any closer, Trip."

"Surely you don't think I'm about to commit some blunder and cause—"

"Trip, listen!" she whispered, hugging him and nodding at the door they'd just used.

A murmur of voices was coming from the other side of the door.

Then, very slowly, the handle began to turn.

Chapter 27

Bubber Kapusky glanced down at the trousers he'd just stepped free of. "This sort of discussion, at this time, isn't very—"

"Don't go spoiling the evening by bickering, Bubber." Pam Sitcominsky was sitting on the edge of the bed in his suite at the Ziggyland Hotel. She was wearing pale tan panty hose and nothing else. "Hurry up, and then it'll be my turn."

Kicking his pants aside, the CIA agent told her, "I took a shower already today."

"What time was that?"

"This morning, right after I got up."

"Eight o'clock, damn it. Thirteen minutes after."

"Well, that was more than a dozen hours ago, Bubber. You've been schlepping all over LA since, picking up all sorts of germs, toxic—"

"I've been here in Ziggyland most of the day. It's notorious for being one of the neatest, cleanest spots on the face of—''

''You were also at Mother Scum's,'' she reminded him.

''Yes, where I paid nearly fifty bucks for coffee and doughnuts.''

''You didn't pay for it, it goes on your expense account.'' When she leaned toward him, her handsome breasts slapped gently together. ''Now go take your shower, so you'll be antiseptically clean when we make love.''

''I really think, in my heart, Pam, that I'm as antiseptically clean as I need to be right now already.''

''Bubber, dearest, we live in the AIDS era and . . . by the way, what sort of soap do you use?''

''It says Ziggyland Hotel on the wrapper and has pictures of Ronny and Fanny Rat on it,'' he said, gesturing in the direction of the bathroom he was not anxious to enter. ''I found six tiny bars and two plastic glasses on the sink when I checked in this—''

''That'll never do.'' She stretched out across the width of the bed, reached over the far side for her discarded purse. ''Use this bar of Dr. Marcus's Genuine Germkiller Offical Hospital Soap.'' She tossed him an unwrapped bar of dead white soap encased in a plastic sandwich bag.

He let it sail by, making no effort to catch it. ''Pam, I happen to be an agent of the United States government,'' he told her slowly and evenly. ''I undergo regular and very thorough medical exams. I can assure you that I don't have any—not *one*—communicable social diseases.''

''When was your last checkup?''

''Four months ago.''

''Four whole months? Do you have any idea how many

dread diseases and blights you could've contracted in that time?''

He sighed. ''While we were tearing off each other's clothes, only moments ago,'' he said, ''I got the foolish notion we were going to hop into bed and—''

''We are, if you'll stop acting dopey, march in, and take your shower,'' she said, sitting up. ''Oh, and be sure to scrub all your intimate areas extra well with Dr. Marcus's soap so that—''

The bedside phone rang.

After booting his discarded trousers once more, Kapusky went over and answered it. ''Yeah?''

''This is Agent Rick Martin, sir.''

''So?''

''Something's happening.''

''Am I to guess?''

''No, I'm going to tell you.''

''Good. I look forward to that.''

''Okay. Triple 'O' Seven and Emily Watts-Batsfree slipped out of their suite here in the hotel approximately seventeen minutes ago.''

''And went where, Martin?''

''Into the sewer system.''

''Damn, sounds like they're heading into the underground sector of Ziggyland. They must know something we don't.''

''That's what we assume, Chief. Shall we pursue?''

''Alert six agents and wait for me in the damn lobby,'' ordered Kapusky. ''I'll be down in ten minutes to supervise this.'' He hung up.

''Sounds as though,'' said Pam, ''you're going to be busy.''

"This may not take more than a few hours." Bending, he retrieved his trousers. "Take your shower and go through whatever other medical procedures are necessary. By the time you're ready, I ought to be back."

Dr. Maybe tugged at his brother's jacket. "I don't really think this is very wise."

"I'm in a tourist mood." He twisted the door handle further, pushing the door open.

"Tomorrow's the big day, our most important test yet and you're wandering around in pursuit of your . . . um . . . hobby."

Dr. Yes pushed on in to the Robotics Lab. "I don't intend to *eat* Bud Ziggy, brother," he assured Dr. Maybe, who followed him reluctantly inside. "The man is respected and loved throughout the civilized world. Besides, I don't like frozen food."

"Very well. You take a quick look at him, and then we have to trot along to the storeroom. There's still a lot of work to be done tonight."

"We're basically executive types." Dr. Yes strolled between the worktables, heading toward the alcove and the glass coffin. "Others can do the work."

Maybe had halted and was gazing around at the equipment and then at the fourteen or so figures lined up along the wall. "I'm used to my body," he remarked.

"So are a lot of other fellows."

"No, I mean, I don't think it would be at all pleasant to have your brain transplanted into one of these robot bodies, the way they're supposed to do with Bud Ziggy's brain eventually."

Yes had reached the alcove and was standing looking

down at the frozen corpse of Bud Ziggy. "It would really depend on how well your mechanical body duplicated various functions."

"You mean, you're wondering if a robot eats?"

"Exactly. Be no fun to live forever if there were no more meals to enjoy."

"I wonder if they build them with . . . um . . . sexual organs." He crossed over to the white-suited Mark Twain. "A future without one's private parts would be bleak indeed."

Dr. Yes clasped his hands behind his back, studying the body in the glass coffin. "From the pictures and videotapes I've seen, I expected Bud Ziggy to be a bit plumper."

"Twain doesn't."

"Twain doesn't what?"

"Have any sexual equipment."

"He's a literary figure. He doesn't need any."

Dr. Maybe moved on along the line. "An eternity without a putz, though, is rather unsettling to contemplate."

"I could do without that, but not without a stomach."

"This is interesting."

"What is?" inquired his brother from across the wide laboratory.

"Well, here's a robot that's a dead ringer for that Triple 'O' Seven chap."

"What park attraction can he be meant for?"

"Perhaps they're going to add some sort of espionage ride." Dr. Maybe moved closer to the figure. "I bet they've built him, from what I've heard of his reputation, with all the sexual parts." He reached out. "I'll check it out."

Bop!

A fist had come hurtling at the Oriental's chin. It connected solidly. His teeth clicked, his eyes rolled, he toppled rapidly backward. He hit into the nearest lab table, knocked over a scanner and a soldering iron before falling to the floor unconscious.

Dr. Yes spun around, and reached inside his jacket for a weapon.

Emily, who'd been impersonating a robot two places down from Seven, got to her thigh holster first and fired her Glock 17 automatic at Dr. Yes.

Kachow!

Her first shot missed him but connected with the glass coffin.

There was a loud shattering sound as part of the lid broke into jagged chunks and went flying. Next came the hiss of escaping air.

Emily fired again, just as Yes brought his Heckler & Koch P7-M8 automatic pistol into view.

Kachow!

Her second shot caught him in the chest. He bellowed in pain, tried to aim his gun and squeeze its trigger. He failed.

A glanging alarm, no doubt set off because damage had been done to Bud Ziggy's coffin, had started to ring loudly all around them and out in the corridors as well.

Dr. Yes hit the floor and stayed there.

"Come on," said Seven, stepping around the fallen Dr. Maybe, "let's get to that storeroom before the Ziggyland security people arrive on the scene."

"I feel absolutely dreadful." Emily ran toward the door with him. "It's you who has the reputation for this sort of thing and yet it was I who futzed up Bud Ziggy's final resting place. Do you think they'll be able to salvage his body?''

''Probably not,'' he said as they dashed along the gray corridor. ''But don't worry, Emily, whatever damage has been done—everyone will blame on me.''

Chapter 28

SOMEWHERE OVER THE PACIFIC

The small private jet was winging its way through the darkening evening sky. Triple 'O' Seven was in the pilot seat, frowning at the controls. "I wish V had briefed me more thoroughly on this new experimental ship of Z's."

Emily was in the copilot seat, wiping at some damp spots on the knees of her jeans with a paper towel. "The coffee dispenser button ought to be more clearly labeled."

"Decidedly, and the nozzle in a different location."

After giving her thigh a pat, she discarded the wadded-up towel and eyed Seven. "You didn't simply feign clumsiness to make me feel better?"

"Do I look the sort of chap who thinks a lapful of hot coffee would cheer a person up?"

"What I mean is, you didn't feign this to take my mind off my own clumsiness at Ziggyland the day before yesterday?"

"I was looking for the wing light button."

"It's right there," she said, pointing, "marked *wing lights*."

"Ah yes, so it is." He pushed it. "My advice, Emily, is that you forget the negative aspects of our adventures under Ziggyland. We did, after all, thwart an unscrupulous plan to infect untold thousands with uncontrollable lust."

"But, Trip, I thawed Bud Ziggy."

"They may be able, from what I was able to learn, to freeze him again."

"A man who is still worshiped by millions of children around the—"

"There isn't even any guarantee that they can ever revitalize his brain anyway," he reminded her. "So even if you hadn't shot a hole in his coffin while saving my life, he might never—"

"Even so, I feel badly. And I'm wondering . . . well, I suppose that's foolish."

"You're wondering if my clumsiness is contagious?"

"No, wondering if my romantic involvement with you has made me less efficient as an agent."

"Romance isn't a handicap. Look at my father's career."

"I should have felled Dr. Yes with my first shot."

"Strive to keep looking on the bright side," he advised as the night closed in around their jet plane. "We incapacitated Dr. Yes and captured Dr. Maybe. By using that new truth spray of Z's on Maybe I was able to find out where Underfoot and the *Pitstop*! manufacturing plant is."

"Yes, but because I shot up the coffin and—"

"One shot is not, technically, shooting it up, Emily."

"Nevertheless, my shot set off alarms that alerted B.

Jobb and he got away—clean away." She made a small forlorn sound. "For all we know he's back on this Hawaiian island we're heading for, readying a trap for us."

"We have to assume that he well may," said Seven. "But then, when one is a secret agent, one has to assume that just about anyone may be setting a trap for one."

She smiled almost sadly at him. "You've been very supportive throughout this whole operation," she said. "Do you think you can put this ship on automatic for a spell?"

"There's a mechanism for that right here on the control panel," he said, glancing at the controls. "Yes, this seems to be the one."

Loud Dixieland music came blaring out of the radio.

"That can't be it, Trip."

He leaned forward, narrowing his eyes. "I see, it's this other gadget. There." He leaned back, relaxing some. "Seems to be flying itself."

"I imagine that bed we noticed back in the passenger cabin works like any other bed." She unbuckled herself from the seat.

"Perhaps you'd best let me try it first." He left his seat and moved to the cabin door. "If it catapults me across the room, we'll know it's another of Z's little inventions."

"Gunk," remarked Bitchy Sue Bedrock.

"Beg pardon, child?" said her father.

"Nothing," she said, setting aside a container of yogurt and leaning back in an armchair in the parlor of their International Toiletries private jet.

"Honey, I'd hate to think that you felt you could no

longer communicate with your old daddy,'' said T.Texas Bedrock. ''I mean to say, you've always come to me with your little problems over the years—the time you shot Baron Chou-Fleur in the south of France, that little episode in Rio with the Archbishop of—''

''I was just merely expressing distaste for my carton of passion fruit yogurt,'' the redhead said. ''And sort of wishing I hadn't gone on this darn diet.''

''You're way too skinny as it is. What you ought to do—not that I'm the kind of father who tells his daughter what she ought to do—but what you ought to do is put on weight, honey, not shed it.''

''If I lose another ten pounds, I'll be even more attractive.''

''Damn, child,'' said the multimillionaire, ''you're cuter than a sour bug's rear end already.''

''Triple 'O' Seven didn't think so.''

''He probably did, honey, and was just too shy to tell you. That's known as British reserve.''

''He jumped in the ocean rather than spend anymore time with me.''

''That's the damn English for you again,'' said Bedrock. ''You offer them a bribe and they blush and run.''

''Nope, I'm sure it was just because he thought I wasn't attractive.''

Her father took a sip of his brandy. ''We more than likely'll run into him when we get to Hawaii,'' he told her. ''So I don't want you to act like some damn schoolgirl with—''

''I have no further interest in him,'' she said disdainfully. ''All I want to do on this trip is help you locate Underfoot and persuade him to sell us his darn formula.''

"Damn shame Seven caught up with them at Ziggyland before they had a chance to test that stuff one more time."

"Father, thousands of innocent people might have suffered if—"

"What's that?" He scowled at her. "Are you developing some kind of moral sense?"

Bitchy Sue shook her head. "No, Pop."

"I hope not." Her father eyed her for a few silent seconds. "You're not still moping over Triple 'O' Seven, are you?"

"I am not," she assured him. "But I do hope he's going to be where we're going."

"Why?"

"I think," she said, "that maybe I'd like to shoot him."

Chapter 29

HAWAII

The tour bus rolled to a stop in a parking lot surrounded by bright tropical foliage. The driver pulled the door release and the dozen passengers filed out into the hazy afternoon sun.

Standing on the pink-tinted asphalt was a pretty young dark-haired woman in grass skirt and flowered halter. "Welcome to Plant number six of the Papp Pineapple Company," she said, smiling around at the group. "I am Moana, your guide on your tour of Papp Pineapple Plant number six. If you'll follow me now we'll begin to find out how pineapple is processed and canned—what we at Papp Pineapple Plant number six like to refer to as the romance of pineapple. Let me caution you in advance not to walk too close to the edge of any of the ramps and catwalks and to be careful not to topple into any of our sanitary vats or . . ."

Emily whispered to Seven as they followed the others,

"I still can't believe B. Jobb has a secret facility under this place."

"That's what Dr. Maybe assured me."

"I know why we're here—to sneak into the hidden lab that's manufacturing Underfoot's mist," she said. "But what are these other people doing here?"

"Papp's is a legitimate tourist attraction on this island." Seven was disguised as a tourist, wearing tan shorts, a multicolored tropical shirt, dark glasses, a wide-brimmed straw hat, and two cameras.

Emily was decked out in similar fashion. "It never occurred to me before that there was any romance to pineapple."

"Then you may learn something this afternoon."

They were at the rear of the line of tourists and the last to enter the factory. It was warm inside the metal-walled building. The air was humid and filled with the odor of cooking pineapple.

In this first large room workers in white uniforms were chopping up whole pineapples, extracting the yellow cores and depositing them on conveyor belts.

"Very romantic," murmured Emily.

"Yes, sure is, Mother." Seven brought up one of his cameras and snapped a few pictures. "Won't the folks back home get a big kick when they see our slides of this." He kept the camera in front of his face as they moved deeper into the plant.

"Something wrong?" asked Emily.

"You ought to take some pictures, too, Mother." In a lowered voice he added, "Dickens Underfoot just came in through that door across the room, and he's got T. Texas Bedrock and his daughter with him."

She lifted a camera, clicked off a shot of a group of pineapples bouncing along toward the next phase. "How did the Bedrocks get here?"

"They've got a very good intelligence gathering setup," he replied. "I imagine Bedrock is here to make Underfoot an offer for his formula."

"Well, we'll be in the next room soon and out of their—"

"Leaping lizards!" came the voice of Bitchy Sue Bedrock above the noise of the pineapple factory. "There's Triple 'O' Seven over yonder dressed up like a dopey tourist!"

"This is really dumb," commented Bitchy Sue as B.J. finished tying her to a straight-backed wooden chair in the underground Underfoot laboratory.

"Perhaps," said the large, white-suited black man. "Yet I have no choice. It's essential to my plans that Triple 'O' Seven and the girl die, so that—"

"Not bad enough he's an evil-hearted villain," said Emily, who was tied securely to a wooden chair next to the securely tied Seven, "but he's also a sexist. Referring to me as a girl and not a woman is—"

"Best not heckle," advised Seven.

"Sir," said the already trussed-up T. Texas Bedrock, "I am noted far and wide in the business community as a master of deceit, a consummate liar, and a champion of duplicity. You have my solemn word that little Bitchy Sue and me'll keep our mouths shut."

"We can't take the chance," said B.J., shaking his head. "Now let me get to the explanation of what Underfoot and I have in mind for you folks."

"Perhaps," cut in Dickens Underfoot, a short, frail man with wavy blond hair, "I'd better fill them in on this technical stuff, B.J."

Jobb shrugged. "I'm pretty good at explaining scientific concepts to laymen, but if you'd rather do it yourself, go ahead."

Underfoot picked up a large unlabeled spray can from atop a white metal lab table. "This contains a much more powerful version of my basic formula. One whiff of this and even the most blasé, indifferent subject becomes inflamed with passion—oh, and by the way, it works both by inhalation and through skin contact. So those of you wearing those little gas masks in your nostrils will be affected. If the subject's overpowering desires are not satisfied, then a condition of extreme frustration develops and, should that not be soon relieved, death will supervene." He held the can higher, chuckling approvingly. "You can imagine that if the subject is tied hand and foot when a substantial dose of this is administered, that a condition of extreme frustration will result. I estimate that none of you will survive beyond eight or nine minutes. Any questions?"

"You're not going to use that gunk on us?" said Bitchy Sue, struggling against the ropes that bound her to the chair.

"I am, Ms. Bedrock, yes."

"But we came here on legit business," she pointed out, "to make a deal to buy a watered-down version of your formula."

"Actually," said Underfoot, "I never had any intention of doing any such thing. But I felt that, since you'd found out where I was based, I must silence you in some—"

"Then even if I hadn't hooted and hollered when I spotted Triple 'O' Seven, you'd have bumped me and my daddy off?"

"Probably," he admitted, "although I might, since I do possess a humane streak, simply have altered your brains so that you wouldn't remember any of—"

"We'll still settle for that," she told him.

"Too late," said B.J. "Get on with it, Underfoot."

"You realize," said Seven, "that my colleague and I are official representatives of the British government. Killing us will look very bad on your record, Underfoot."

The inventor chuckled again, taking a few steps in Seven's direction. "It already is severely stained, and one more blemish won't make much difference."

The blank plaster walls of the underground room suddenly began to shiver and groan.

Scowling, B.J. glanced up at the ceiling. "What the hell's going on?"

The walls shuddered violently. Jagged zigzag cracks began to appear in them. A great rumbling had commenced.

Underfoot dropped the can. "It's Mount Noofu," he cried. "That supposedly extinct volcano is erupting."

"It's not supposed to." B.J. dodged a chunk of plaster that fell down from the ceiling.

"Let's vacate." Underfoot started running for the door, across a floor that was buckling and swaying.

"Hey, you dope!" yelled Bitchy Sue. "Don't leave us in this dump with the walls caving in."

B. Jobb and the scientist ignored her cries and took their leave.

Chapter 30

Impressively large cracks were appearing in the walls; just about everything in the room was jiggling.

"If I can get this chair to topple over," said Seven as he struggled to do that, "I ought to be able to smash it and get free."

"Good luck," said Emily, watching him anxiously. "It just might work."

"Yes, I think I'm—"

Thunk!

He and his chair fell over. The wooden frame hit the concrete floor hard. But the chair frame didn't crack and Seven remained firmly attached to it by the expertly knotted ropes.

"Will you, for cripesakes," said Bitchy Sue, "quit doing tricks and get us the heck out of here. Otherwise we're going to be buried alive."

"Doing the best I can, Miss Bedrock," he replied from the floor.

The ground beneath them was full of rumblings, and the walls were developing an increasing number of cracks.

"Perhaps, Emily," suggested Seven, "you can get your chair to tip over and break."

"I've thought of that, Trip, but I'm too close to this lab table to start it rocking properly."

"Well, let me think . . . Ow! Ouch!"

"What's wrong?"

"My fountain pen smashed in the fall."

"Holy moley," commented Bitchy Sue. "We're on the brink of complete and total oblivion and this gink is kvetching about his darn fountain pen."

"This one's full . . . yow . . . of acid," he explained. "And the acid is eating through my clothes . . . and the ropes!"

A moment later, by striving to move both of his arms away from his sides, he snapped the ropes around his upper body.

"Top hole," said Emily encouragingly.

Swiftly Seven untied the ropes from around his legs and ankles and stood up.

Chunks of ceiling were falling down all around them now.

Getting his pocketknife out, Seven cut Emily free. "Take care of Bedrock and I'll do Bitchy Sue."

"Don't poke me with that darn blade," warned the redhead as he started in on her bonds.

He soon cut the ropes away, yanking her up and out of the chair. "Head for the door."

"I'm afraid the darn ceiling's going to fall on—"

"Come on, we've got to get out of here." He scooped

her off her feet and ran, dodging falling debris. "Coming, Emily?"

"Right behind you, toting Mr. Bedrock."

"My foot's asleep," explained the toiletries tycoon. "Can't walk on it."

Seven got the heavy metal door open with his shoulder. There was a metal stairway beyond it and the steps were somewhat twisted and bent. With Bitchy Sue in his arms he started up.

The door at the top of the fifteen steps led into the pineapple factory.

Seven took three strides across the upper floor, then skidded, swayed, and fell over. "Damn, something sticky all over the floor."

Bitchy Sue had rolled out of his grasp and was sitting in one of the puddles. "It's pineapple juice," she said. "The darn floor's awash with it and hundreds of little pineapple chunks."

Rising, carefully, to his feet, he offered her his hand. "We'll try for that door over there," he said. "It leads to the parking lot."

They started off, and beside them was Emily carrying the incapacitated Bedrock.

Outside the late afternoon sky was a smoky orange. A large crack had opened across the entire lot and the tourist bus had fallen halfway into it.

"Look over there next to the crevice," said Emily as she set the tycoon on his feet.

Seven cautiously approached the figure sprawled out on the jagged ground next to the fallen bus. A heavy palm tree had been uprooted and fallen across the body. "Yes, this is Dickens Underfoot,'' said Seven, crouching. ''The poor chap's dead and done for.''

''Damn it,'' said Bedrock. ''Now I'll never get hold of his formula.''

''Unless,'' said Seven, standing, ''B. J. has a copy.''

''Say, that's an idea. I wonder where he's gotten to.''

Emily was sitting on the balcony of a suite in one of Oahu's finer hotels. She had a phone resting on her knee and was talking to distant London as she looked down at the sun-bright midday beach far below. ''It seems to be definite, yes,'' she said. ''B. Jobb's plane crashed quite near the volcano.''

''Have they recovered his remains?'' inquired P.

''Not as yet, since the ship is under considerable lava.''

''Then it's possible the man is not dead at all.''

''That seems unlikely, sir,'' she answered. ''Jobb was seen, by several tourists who'd been visiting Papp Pineapple, running from the place and getting into the twin-engine plane just as the eruption started. Other reliable witnesses saw the plane go out of control soon thereafter and crash.''

''One wonders how reliable people who've experienced a volcanic upheaval are as witnesses,'' said P. ''Well, for now we'll presume the bloke is defunct.''

''Unless there are further outbreaks of lust,'' Emily said, ''this particular threat to civilization as we know it seems to be over and done with.''

''For now I'll place the Underfoot matter in the inactive file.'' He cleared his throat. ''You might as well tell me about your most recent expenses, Emily.''

"There's really nothing unusual, sir," she assured him. "Fuel for our plane, hotel room here on Oahu, meals, and sundries."

"There was a rumor that a bordello had fallen over on B. Jobb's island. Did Seven have anything to do with that?"

"Not a thing. Nearly all the damage done over on that little island was due to the volcano's acting up."

"Good, since I'd hate to have to justify paying for a bordello."

Emily asked, "Is there anything further on the Bud Ziggy situation?"

P said, "Apparently they have him safely frozen again—called in an expert from a nearby frozen yogurt shop and he showed them how to handle the situation. So far as anyone can tell, Ziggy's brain is in as good condition as it was the day he died."

Emily gave a relieved sigh. "I'm glad to hear that."

"Is Seven there with you?"

"He's taking a shower at the moment."

"He seems to do a great deal of that."

"He says his brief visit to the hospital to treat the acid burn on his chest left him reeking of medicine."

"How serious is the burn?"

"Minor."

P said, "I'd like him to call me when he's free."

"I do hope, sir, you don't intend to criticize him. All in all, you know, I think he's done an admirable job," Emily said. "Especially since the CIA was trying to outfox and sabotage us, and that awful Bedrock woman tried to—"

"Yes, yes. I'm quite pleased with his work on this, and with yours as well," said P. "In fact, I intend to ask Triple 'O' Seven to return to active duty."

Emily frowned. "I rather think he won't."

"You've already, have you, brought up the subject with him?"

"He brought it up," she replied. "My impression is that he would much prefer to return to his teaching career."

"Then it's up to you to persuade him to do otherwise," said P. "Use your feminine wiles if need be."

"Oh, I plan to use them," she said, smiling. "But not for recruiting purposes."

She hung up.

MORE MYSTERIOUS PLEASURES

HAROLD ADAMS		
The Carl Wilcox mystery series		
MURDER	#501	$3.95
PAINT THE TOWN RED	#601	$3.95
THE MISSING MOON	#602	$3.95
THE NAKED LIAR	#420	$3.95
THE FOURTH WIDOW	#502	$3.50
THE BARBED WIRE NOOSE	#603	$3.95
THE MAN WHO MET THE TRAIN	#801	$3.95
TED ALLBEURY		
THE SEEDS OF TREASON	#604	$3.95
THE JUDAS FACTOR	#802	$4.50
THE STALKING ANGEL	#803	$3.95
ERIC AMBLER		
HERE LIES: AN AUTOBIOGRAPHY	#701	$8.95
ROBERT BARNARD		
A TALENT TO DECEIVE: AN APPRECIATION OF AGATHA CHRISTIE	#702	$8.95
EARL DERR BIGGERS		
The Charlie Chan mystery series		
THE HOUSE WITHOUT A KEY	#421	$3.95
THE CHINESE PARROT	#503	$3.95
BEHIND THAT CURTAIN	#504	$3.95
THE BLACK CAMEL	#505	$3.95
CHARLIE CHAN CARRIES ON	#506	$3.95
KEEPER OF THE KEYS	#605	$3.95
JAMES M. CAIN		
THE ENCHANTED ISLE	#415	$3.95
CLOUD NINE	#507	$3.95

BILL PRONZINI

GUN IN CHEEK	#714	$8.95
SON OF GUN IN CHEEK	#715	$9.95

BILL PRONZINI AND JOHN LUTZ

THE EYE	#408	$3.95

ROBERT J. RANDISI, ED.

THE EYES HAVE IT: THE FIRST PRIVATE EYE WRITERS OF AMERICA ANTHOLOGY	#716	$8.95
MEAN STREETS: THE SECOND PRIVATE EYE WRITERS OF AMERICA ANTHOLOGY	#717	$8.95
AN EYE FOR JUSTICE: THE THIRD PRIVATE EYE WRITERS OF AMERICA ANTHOLOGY	#729	$9.95

PATRICK RUELL

RED CHRISTMAS	#531	$3.50
DEATH TAKES THE LOW ROAD	#532	$3.50
DEATH OF A DORMOUSE	#636	$3.95

HANK SEARLS

THE ADVENTURES OF MIKE BLAIR	#718	$8.95

DELL SHANNON

The Lt. Luis Mendoza mystery series

CASE PENDING	#211	$3.95
THE ACE OF SPADES	#212	$3.95
EXTRA KILL	#213	$3.95
KNAVE OF HEARTS	#214	$3.95
DEATH OF A BUSYBODY	#315	$3.95
DOUBLE BLUFF	#316	$3.95
MARK OF MURDER	#417	$3.95
ROOT OF ALL EVIL	#418	$3.95

RALPH B. SIPPER, ED.

ROSS MACDONALD'S INWARD JOURNEY	#719	$8.95

JULIE SMITH

The Paul McDonald mystery series

TRUE-LIFE ADVENTURE	#407	$3.95
HUCKLEBERRY FIEND	#637	$3.95

The Rebecca Schwartz mystery series

TOURIST TRAP	#533	$3.95

ROSS H. SPENCER

THE MISSING BISHOP	#416	$3.50
MONASTERY NIGHTMARE	#534	$3.50

VINCENT STARRETT

THE PRIVATE LIFE OF SHERLOCK HOLMES	#720	$8.95